SCORPIO

Book 3

Descending

ALEX McDONOUGH

iBooks
Habent Sua Fata Libelli

iBooks
Manhanset House
Shelter Island Hts., New York 11965-0342

bricktower@aol.com • www.ibooksinc.com

Library of Congress Cataloging-in-Publication Data
McDonough, Alex.
Scorpio Descending
p. cm.

1. Fiction—Science Fiction—Time Travel.
2. Fiction—Science Fiction—Alien Contact.
3. Fiction—Romance—Time Travel.
Fiction, I. Title.

978-1-59687-670-5, Trade Paper

Developed by Byron Preiss
Editor: Gillian Bucky
Cover Painting by John Jude Palencar
Map by John Pierard
Special thanks to Janet Fox

January 2024

SCORPIO

Book 3

Descending

ALEX McDONOUGH

Books in the *Scorpio Series*

Scorpio

Scorpio Rising

Scorpio Descending

Scorpio Dragon's Blood

Scorpio Dragon's Eye

Scorpio Dragon's Claw

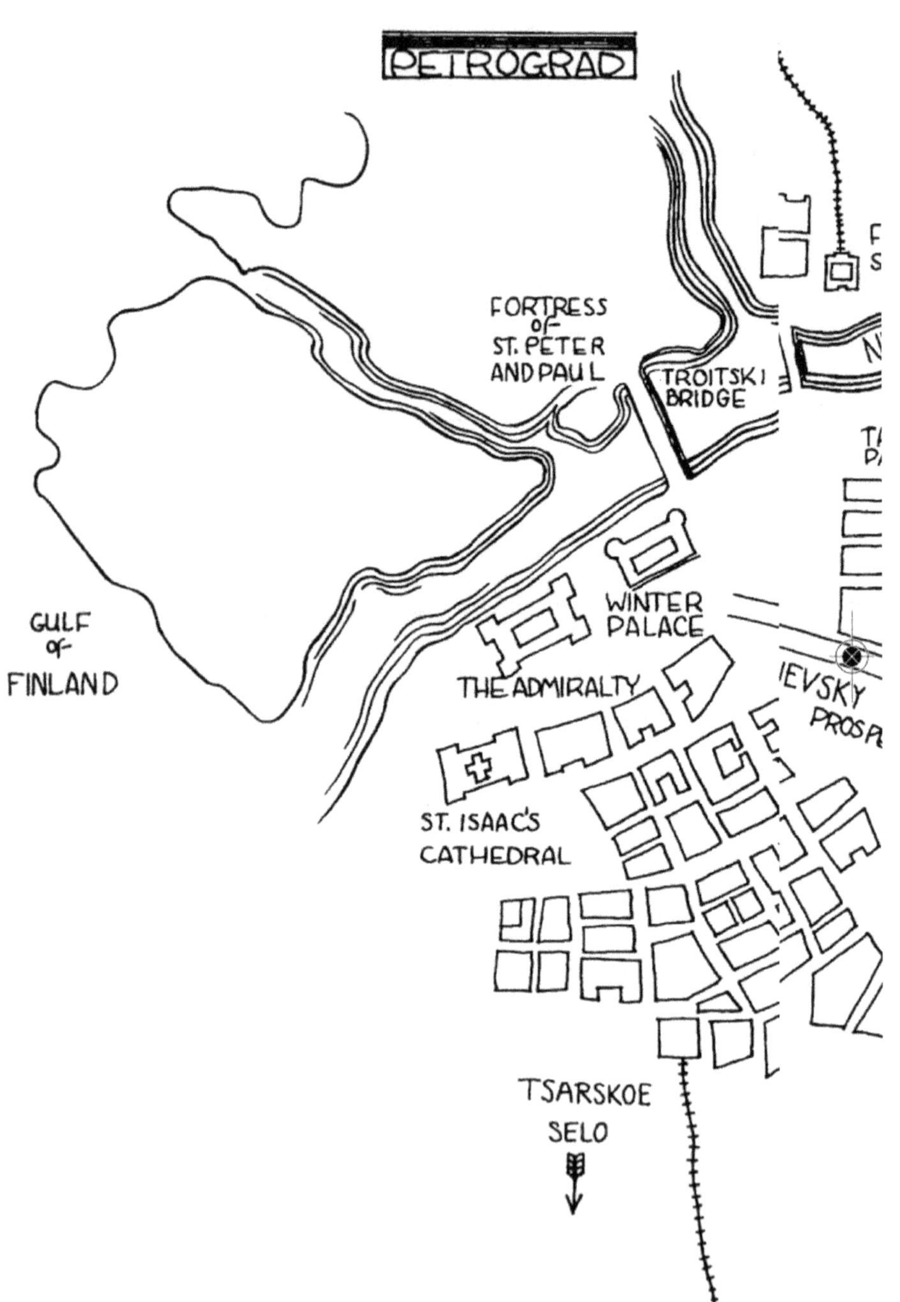
PETROGRAD
FORTRESS of ST. PETER AND PAUL
TROITSKI BRIDGE
WINTER PALACE
GULF of FINLAND
THE ADMIRALTY
ST. ISAAC'S CATHEDRAL
TSARSKOE SELO

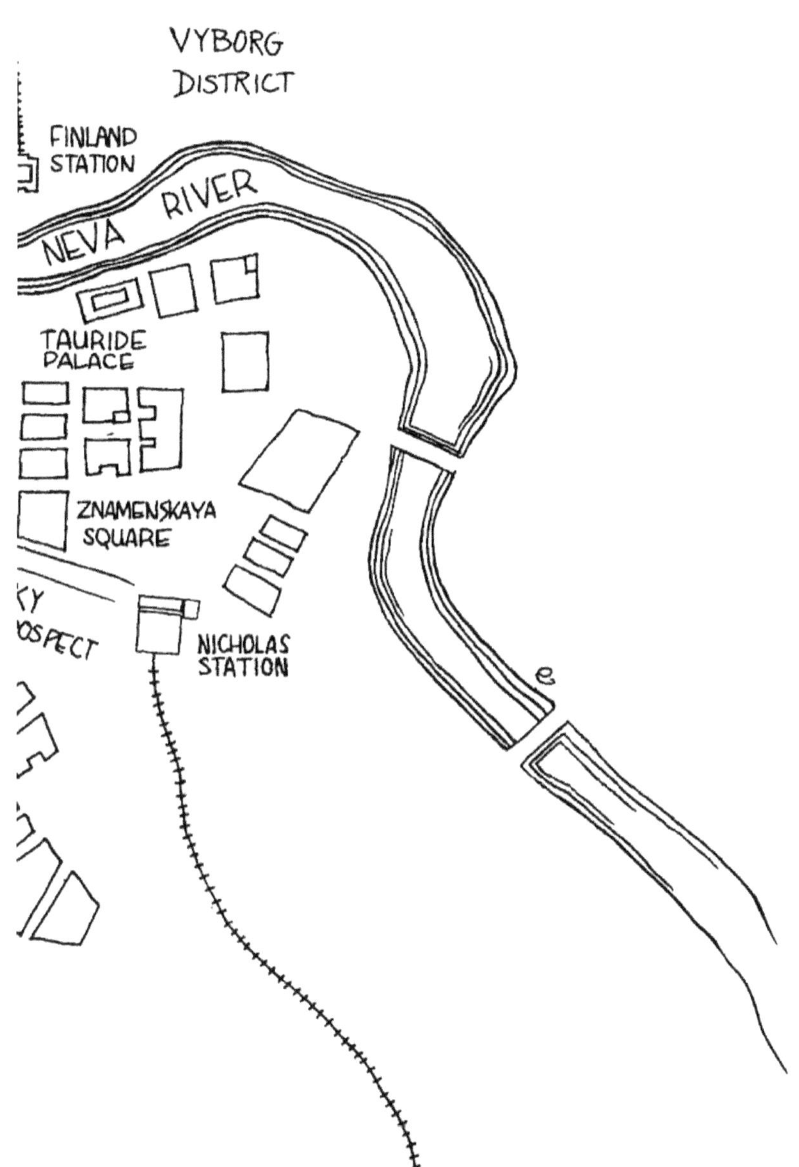
VYBORG
DISTRICT
FINLAND
STATION
NEVA RIVER
TAURIDE
PALACE
ZNAMENSKAYA
SQUARE
NICHOLAS
STATION

Leah awoke with a start to gunfire and shouts. Remembering the raid on the apartment building, she leaped from bed. Only when she was ready to escape did she creep to the window and peer out.

Mobs of soldiers were running through the streets, firing in the air and shouting. Men ran from doorways to join them. A car crammed with soldiers careened around a corner. Long red banners had been tied to their bayonets and streamed out behind.

After a moment she realized someone had been pounding on her door for some time. Radek didn't look as if he'd slept all night; his hair was tousled and his eyes red-rimmed.

"We've done it!" he shouted. "Early this morning the soldiers held a secret meeting and voted to mutiny. They shot the commander who ordered them to fire on their own people, and went out urging other regiments to join them. The whole army is in chaos. The revolution has begun!"

Table of Contents

Prologue

Leah de Bernay floated in orb space beyond the normal concept of space and time, her thoughts and feelings drifting past her in bright but swiftly fading dream images and snippets of memory. It was surprising to realize that not only was she not alone in the bubblelike craft, her thoughts and feelings weren't entirely her own. Her companion was an alien, Scorpio, from the world called Terrapin, and while drifting together in this realm between space and time, their minds tended to leak ideas and emotions, until it was hard to tell where Scorpio ended and Leah began.

This strange communion didn't frighten her, because she and Scorpio had voyaged together before. In orb space they were as one, but when the craft landed, they were separate again, except for a lingering but somewhat tenuous ability to read each other's minds.

She began to feel homesick for green seas lapping at crystalline beaches and wanted to dive into the deeps where the water was chill and bracing. No, that wasn't right. Somewhere inside her mind Scorpio was laughing at her. She had come from the sprawling city of Avignon in the fourteenth century. Her father had been a respected doctor and they had lived in the Jewish sector. She had expected to live out an uneventful life there, until Scorpio had landed, bearing a time-traveling orb and bringing trouble in his wake.

She and Scorpio remembered together how it had been on Terrapin when the Hunters attempted to destroy Scorpio's people, the Aquay. Though he was one of the few of his naturally timid race who fought back, two Hunters had taken an oath to kill him. The orb, which he had stolen from the Hunters, was Scorpio's one chance to help his people survive, but there was also one small problem: he didn't know how to control it. Their last stop had been Elizabethan England, but when the Hunters had appeared, they were forced to jump blindly into the time stream. They could emerge anywhere, anywhen at all.

Chapter One

Through the rapidly dissolving skin of the orb bubble that had enclosed her, Leah saw an alien landscape: wind-eroded dunes of snow swirled around the rugged boles of close-grown trees. These trees were ancient monsters with thick, shaggy bark, moss growing in clumps on their shadow sides. The sky, what she could see of it past the tops of the trees, was a blue so intense it hurt. Her first sensation, once the orb bubble had burst, was cold. Not any cold she had ever been exposed to; this was a fierce, killing cold. Breathing made her lungs tingle. The air was pure as crystal, causing her perversely to long for the close-packed human stench of Avignon or London. She pulled the thin cloth of her barmaid's garb closer around her, noticing the charred places on the skirt. The Hunter's laser blast had been a near-miss. In the haste of their flight she hadn't had time to be afraid, but now their narrow escape seemed like a nightmare.

"Where can we be? I wonder," said Scorpio aloud. Leah noticed he wasn't shivering and dancing from foot to foot as she was. "I find this climate somewhat invigorating," he said.

She supposed the thick gray skin that had allowed him to swim in the depths of a lake without feeling the cold made him more at home here. If home was the sort of word that applied, she thought ruefully, seeing only more immense trees and drifts of snow in all directions. There was nothing in sight that looked as if it had been built by man.

"I'm afraid the orb has taken us to some uninhabited world," said Leah. "Or a time before people existed. Maybe we should consider jumping again." She said this reluctantly, knowing that Scorpio had no control over the orb. They might as easily end up in the middle of an ocean or a place more desolate than this.

Scorpio looked at the orb. As it had after their first long jump, it looked slightly withered, and the golden aura about it had a greenish cast. Whatever powers it drew upon to move them through time and space seemed weaker after a jump.

"We don't know anything about this place yet," said Scorpio. "Maybe it would be better to explore a little before giving up on it so soon. This may only be an uninhabited area."

"I'm too cold to care," said Leah through chattering teeth.

Scorpio looked at her quizzically. "I'm sorry," he said. "I'd forgotten that you humans are more vulnerable to cold temperatures than we Aquay. But we don't have to leave yet. I see shelter just beyond the trees." He loped off through the drifts, giving Leah no choice but to follow.

Ahead, in an outcropping of boulders, she saw a narrow triangular opening half screened by brush. Scorpio slid his skinny shape into the entrance and disappeared. Leah had to squeeze through, scraping her back and sides on the rock, but once inside, she found that the place wasn't so bad, except for a strong musky smell that permeated it.

"Like a home away from home," said Scorpio, placing the orb in a niche in the rocks. There its light waxed and waned like a guttering lamp. The golden light slowly turned an eerie green in the dimness. Leah thought there was something almost desperate in the orb's flickering, as if it were trying to signal something.

"We can't just huddle here in a cave," said Leah.

"You were the one who was cold," said Scorpio. "I thought maybe you could stay here while I look around."

"Fine," said Leah, "you go look around, and when you discover that there's nothing here except ice and snow and trees, we can jump again."

"All right, if that's all I find, I promise we'll go." Something soft bumped against Leah's legs and she screamed. Scorpio reached down and picked up the small gray animal. As it wiggled in his grasp, Leah's first thought was how puppylike and adorable it was. Then a second later she realized it was a wolf cub.

"Scorpio, we've got to get out of here!"

"But this little fellow won't hurt us."

Somewhere in the distance, over the whine of wind, came the keening of a wolf pack.

"No, but it sounds like his mama is coming home, and I don't want to be here when she does!"

She snatched the orb from its resting place and handed it to Scorpio. Forgetting about the cold outside, she wriggled back through the opening. More wolf calls echoed through the cold air, nearer now. She hesitated, trying to decide which way they could safely flee. Hearing Scorpio behind her and trusting that he could keep up, she picked a direction and began to run.

A fine skiff of snow had begun to fall as she floundered through the drifts. The first wolf shape she saw was an insubstantial gray ghost as it paced her through the trees. Grandmère Zarah had told her tales of winters when wolves had become bold enough to prowl the perimeters of Avignon, but though she had once caught a glimpse of one of the shy creatures, wolves were more legend than fact to her.

This wolf was big, shaggy and indisputably real despite the veils of snow that wreathed him. He ran with mouth open, in a canine grin, tongue lolling. A moment later she realized what he was grinning about. Ahead shapes moved to cut off their escape route.

"No use." She turned back to Scorpio, panting so that she could hardly talk. "We've got to jump again."

Scorpio held out the orb and Leah put her hands on it. There was something chill and lifeless about its feel and only a pale light leaked out between their fingers. Leah braced herself for the jolt when reality would recede, but it never came. The forest with its gathering shadows was unmoved. A wolf sat on its haunches, cocking its head to one side, as if trying to figure out their odd actions.

The light showing between their interlaced fingers flickered and went out.

"What's wrong with it?" asked Leah.

"The jump and this cold," said Scorpio. "Maybe it was too much. Maybe we've destroyed the orb. We'll be stuck here forever."

"For us that might not be such a long time," said Leah.

There was something frighteningly efficient in the way the pack had chased and then outmaneuvered them. Now a half dozen of the huge beasts closed in from all directions, with loping movements that seemed almost leisurely. But just when Leah had given up all hope, the wolves stopped, keeping their places in an irregular ring a few yards away. Leah looked at Scorpio. "I think you smell different to them," she said. "They're afraid."

Scorpio tested this by taking a few steps forward. The wolves nearest him gave ground. He began to run toward them, waving his hands, but though they would turn tail and run a short distance, they always stopped again, showing no signs of leaving.

"We're safe for now," said Leah, "but only until they figure out that you're not a real danger to them."

The minutes stretched out with nothing happening, but at last the wolves began to move cautiously toward Scorpio. Leah picked up a branch, and as a shaggy head moved toward her, she swung with all her might. The branch broke across the beast's skull and it staggered away, leaving a trail of blood drops in the snow. Others quickly took its place.

Two short, sharp reports broke the forest's silence, and a wolf dropped. Leah looked around in confusion as the pack broke and ran. She could hardly credit that the shaggy, only vaguely human shape approaching had had anything to do with the wolf lying dead in the snow. It must be magic of the sort the Hunters used when they set her skirt on fire from a distance. She noticed that the figure carried a long sticklike implement and a trace of smoke curled from one end of it.

"We're rescued!" she shouted at Scorpio.

"Are you sure? These animals walk upright, but don't look that much different from the ones that were chasing us."

"They're men," said Leah, without being quite sure of it herself until the figure had approached close enough so that she could see his round, red-cheeked human face, wreathed in a fur hood. As they approached, Leah shouted a welcome, but the words died on her lips as the taller man reached into his coat and drew out a long, sharp knife.

Vasily Andreyovitch Mishkin shouted in triumph as he saw the wolf fall dead in the snow from his shot, but his brother Misha shouted and waved his rifle at the same time. That was just like Misha, he thought. Always ready to lay claim to what rightfully belonged to him. "Plainly it was my shot that brought the beast down," he said.

"The snow must have blurred your vision, Vasha, because I marked that it was my shot that felled the wolf." They confronted each other angrily, looking very much alike: large men, their faces round and red with cold, brushy black beards jutting over and blending with their fur coats.

Vasha was the older, the more gaunt, his lips set in a rigid line. He thought of Misha as the baby, though in truth they were both past thirty. He nursed resentments from when the two of them were but toddlers, and could recall every slight, every time his family passed over him to give the "baby" his way. And yet neither had married, but had continued the free hunting and trapping life with only each other as companion.

The wolf they had just killed came at the end of a long day's hunt that had left Vasha exhausted and discouraged. Surely there was a better life than tramping these woods for days, only to be cheated by the fur buyer and robbed of most of what was left by the Tsar's greedy tax collectors. That was the trouble with the world today, he thought, as he and Misha wallowed through the snow, clumsy in their furs. There was no longer any way for a bold man such as himself to build his fortune. Everything was gnawed away by the bureaucrats.

The windblown veils of snow did make seeing difficult. As he approached the wolf, unlimbering his big skinning knife, he saw two people standing over the fallen animal. No, not two people, he amended. Misha stared at them like a butcher-stunned calf, though he could hardly blame him. The one on the right wasn't recognizably human, and his skinny shape was covered in thick gray skin. From the thin clothing it wore it didn't feel the cold. The other was more mundane, if you didn't wonder how a pretty, dark-haired, skimpily clad young woman had appeared in the wilderness.

Misha was fishing under his furs and hastily brought out the icon painted on a medallion that Grandmother had given him (I *should have received it, as eldest,* Vasha thought). Misha held the icon out before him as if in protection from the outlandish figure.

"B-brother, what manner of creatures do you think these could be?" he asked. "Will they harm us?"

The gray one came forward a step, making Misha wave the icon all the faster. He held out gray, long-fingered hands as if demonstrating his lack of weapons. The vestigial webs between the fingers were more pronounced than in a human hand and the fingertips were spatulate and nailless, the sight making Vasha's flesh crawl. The woman stared at him with wide, dark eyes.

Vasha only now remembered that he still held the long skinning knife. "I believe … they are afraid of us," said Vasha, fumbling to put the knife back into its sheath beneath his coat.

The gray one continued walking toward them and opened its beaklike mouth as if it would speak. Vasha nearly fell backward when the words that emerged were perfectly understandable. He even used the dialect of Tutalsk, Vasha's own village.

"We mean no harm," said Scorpio. "Can you help us?"

"Vasha, it talks."

"Do you think I cannot hear it talking?"

"What do you think it is?"

"I think I do not know what it is."

"Can't you understand us? We need help!" shouted the young woman.

"I think she's human, anyway," said Misha. "She even looks blue from cold." He quickly divested himself of his fur coat and offered it to her. She didn't hesitate, but quickly wrapped herself in it, almost disappearing in its folds.

"What are you doing out here in the taiga?" asked Vasha, his hands indicating the forest all around them. "Where did you come from?"

"We landed here in our orb-craft, but there's something wrong with it," said the gray man before his companion put her fingers to her lips, as if warning him not to say too much.

"But what do you think?" persisted Misha, turning to his brother.

"I think that Lazerev would know," said Vasha.

"Yes, Igor Dmitrovitch is the wisest man in the village," agreed Misha. "I was just about to suggest that myself."

Vasha fumed as Misha invited the two strangers to accompany them. That was just like Misha, he thought. He would tell people in the village that he alone had discovered the gray man.

"Can't you tell us where we are?" asked Scorpio.

"Why you're only seven miles from the village of Tutalsk," said Misha.

Leah and Scorpio exchanged puzzled glances.

"Siberia," said Vasha. Turning to his brother, he added, "Of course they've never heard of our small village, you dullard."

"And the time ... the year," asked Leah.

"Ah, that is easy," said Misha. "November, 1916."

"Are you going to pass the time with our friends or help me skin out this wolf I killed?" said Vasha.

"I'll help, but let's remember whose shot brought it down," said Misha.

• • •

The troika had been left at the top of a nearby hill. The three heavy-coated horses stamped and snorted plumes of breath into the cold air as the brothers helped the two into the sled. Vasha felt a suppressed excitement as he took the reins; the gray man and the girl were an exciting discovery. Nothing like them had ever been seen in Tutalsk. There should be some way a clever man like himself could turn it to his own advantage ...

Waves of fatigue washed over Leah as she snuggled into the heavy fur coat. She heard the jingling of bells on the harness as the three horses raced across the snow. They were fastened to the sled in an odd way, she noticed, one horse running straight ahead, the others moving out at an angle to either side, but they kept the sled moving at a brisk pace, and most of the time, except for a rhythmic swaying, their progress was very smooth. She was sure that before the journey was over she would be asleep, and she didn't know if that would be a good idea or not. The taller man had looked so fierce at first with his huge knife.

Siberia, he had said. She tried to remember her father's geography lessons, but nothing registered. Obviously, he hadn't considered it an important place. Considering what she'd seen of it, she didn't either. 1916. Strange, she'd expected further developments from what she'd seen in Elizabethan England. This land seemed even more primitive than that one, as if time had moved backward. But she didn't know everything about time, she realized. She didn't know anything, and with the orb damaged she was now unlikely to. And she had better learn to like this place. It might become their permanent home. Her head lolled forward, the rocking motion of the sled had put her to sleep.

Chapter Two

The sled hit a bump and Leah awoke with a start. She had forgotten where she was, and when she was. Her dreams all seemed to lead her home, and she had to shake off a heavy feeling of nostalgia as she looked around and saw, except for the Mishkin brothers, the first sign that this world was inhabited. The road was a winding track of snow, hard-packed, but cut and gouged by the runners of sleighs.

"Where are we going?" Leah shouted over the whine of the wind.

"We're taking you to the house of Igor Dmitrovich Lazarev. He's the village shaman and healer, a very old and wise man."

"If he's really so wise, maybe he'll know something about the orb," said Scorpio.

He was only a voice emerging from the fur robe the brothers had thrown over him, though he had never complained of the cold. "Don't be too disappointed if their wise man is just a doddering old goat," said Leah, leaning closer to Scorpio and lowering her voice so the brothers wouldn't hear. "Growing to an old age in this country is probably considered an admirable feat in itself."

Snow was still sifting down ahead of them, moving on the wind and obscuring the countryside with moving veils of white.

"Is the climate always like this?" asked Leah. "Are there always these storms?"

"Storms," laughed Misha. "She calls this a storm."

"This is nothing," said Vasily. "We have three kinds of storms in Siberia. The *miatjel* is a bit worse than this, but no real problem. The *samjots* is a storm of snow and fierce, cold winds, and only experienced travelers should venture out. But when the *wingo* arrives, that's the time to stay in your home and pile up the firewood."

"I have seen a sleigh and driver dug out of the snow after the *wingo* had passed," said Misha. "The horse still standing on its feet, the driver's hands frozen to the reins."

Leah shivered as she imagined the gruesome sight.

At last they pulled up before a small house rudely made of split logs with the bark still on them. A warped thatch roof looked like the nest of some gargantuan bird. The house was so antique and organic it appeared to have grown there, along with the rest of the forest.

As they approached, Vasha stood up in the sled and shouted, *"Diedushka*, it is I, Vasily Andreyovitch, and my brother Mikhail. You know us well!"

Leah expected a withered and gnarled old man to creep out, but the person who came through the door was taller than either of the brothers, broad and muscular, with skin weathered a deep bronze. His luxuriant hair and beard were pure white and, save for creases about his eyes and mouth, the only indication of advanced age. He strode toward the sleigh as Leah was about to alight, grasped her about the waist and swung her easily to the ground. *If he has lived ninety years*, she thought, *he looks ready to live ninety more.*

"One hardly expects guests in midwinter, Vasily Andreyovitch," he said. "Let alone young female ones. And … what have we here?" His attention was now fully on Scorpio and he narrowed his dark eyes.

"That is what we came to ask you, *Diedushka,"* said Misha, calling Igor "grandfather" deferentially because of the man's extreme age. "Surely nothing like this has been seen in the village. We found these two wandering in the wilderness with no indication of how they came to be there."

"Do either of our guests speak?" asked Igor. "Why not just ask them?"

"I tried to tell you earlier about our orb—" began Scorpio, but was silenced by a glare from Leah. Scorpio was as yet under the impression that people wanted a truthful explanation. Leah knew that the truth was likely to be disbelieved or to get them into more trouble.

"Yes, he tried to tell us an outlandish tale of coming from another world," said Vasily, "in some sort of magical craft, which is now damaged so they may not return. We were not so stupid as to believe that."

"A trickster, are you?" asked Igor with a twinkle in his eye as he looked toward Scorpio. "I think there's only one thing he can be, Vasily Andreyovitch. Your grandfather may have told you of the *Lesovik."*

"My grandfather only told me to find honest work and stop loitering about his house," said Vasha as Misha laughed.

"Well, they are old tales, and they say the old tales are truest. The *Lesovik* was a forest spirit that loved to trick those passing through. He was especially fond of carrying away pretty young ladies to be his companions."

Misha nodded vigorously.

Leah breathed an inaudible sigh of relief. In her travels with Scorpio, she had discovered it was better to be silent and let people come to their own conclusions about who and what the being was.

"But no one has seen one of your forest spirits for generations. Why should he appear among us now?" asked Vasily.

"Who knows. My grandfather always told me that the elder spirits would return in troubled times, and walk the earth again," said Igor.

"That makes sense," said Misha. "These are unsettled times. The Tsar passes hard laws. And now he has involved us in a war with Germany, making things worse. The peasants talk about revolt, of taking the land." He gestured toward the sleigh. "Come, we must hurry. Wait until the villagers see that we've captured a *Lesovik.*"

Scorpio looked about with alarm, as if ready to panic. Leah didn't like the idea of being on display either, but there didn't seem much they could do about it.

"Wait, brother," said Vasily. "I'm not sure the village is ready for the sight of this mythological beast. The Tsar's agent would also have many questions to ask us and he might very well decide to take us and these beings into custody, since no one can explain their appearance here."

"I never thought of that," said Misha.

"Only a few come here, and it's remote enough from the village so that their presence could remain a secret," said Vasily. "If it is agreeable with you, *Diedushka*, perhaps the *Lesovik* and his companion could stay here for now?"

"Certainly, it would be a pleasure. I seldom have guests, only those few villagers who seek me out for my philters and remedies, and there seem to be fewer of these all the time, since these 'modern doctors' have come to Irkutsk." He said "modern doctors" as if the words had a bad taste.

"But remember, we're the ones who found them."

"I will not forget," said Igor. "Consider them temporarily in my safekeeping."

After the brothers had driven away, Igor invited Leah and Scorpio to come inside. The small house had little furniture: a wooden table and some benches and these hugged the walls, leaving an open space in the middle. Walls and beams were of unfinished wood, gone iron-dark from age. Beautifully painted religious icons with candles blazing before them were hung in a corner. Igor would later tell her that this was the "Red Corner," but red was a synonym of beautiful in this language, and it only meant that this corner was a spot of beauty in the house. Items with a more primitive look—crude masks of carven wood daubed with red pigment, skin bags embellished with feathers, animal teeth and claws—hung on the other walls. It was as if the old man wasn't taking any chances of offending a deity, either past or present.

Igor led the way to the kitchen that was dominated by a large stove or oven made of brick about four feet high by five long. Kitchenware and foodstuffs occupied a series of niches in one wall. Igor opened the oven door and brought out an iron kettle.

"There is always kasha for whoever may wander past," he said. "Poor fare, I suppose, but I share what I have." He handed them each a wooden spoon, so they wouldn't have to take turns dipping from the kettle. They didn't object because by this time they were very hungry.

Igor sat watching them shrewdly as they ate. Leah discovered that the kasha was a sort of porridge, made from buckwheat. Nourishing, she supposed, if bland.

From a battered metal vessel Igor poured hot water into clay cups.

"So that's a samovar," said Leah softly, as if to herself. When the orb deposited them in a new time and place, it also taught them the language that would be needed. The problem was that at first, their minds would be full of words that didn't seem to mean anything. Only when the corresponding item appeared did the words make sense.

"Of course," said Igor impatiently. "What else would it be?"

She would see different versions of the samovar everywhere, from this one of dented metal to those made of polished brass. It was simply a tube within a tube. Hot coals were shoveled into the central tube and the outer section was filled with water to be heated for tea, a drink that she would discover fueled the entire populace. Usually a pot of strong tea sat atop the samovar, to be diluted with the hot water.

"Thanks for taking us in," said Scorpio. "The two who found us were kind, but I was a little afraid of them."

"They're rough and somewhat ignorant, but mean no harm. You told them you flew here in a strange craft. Is it still in the forest? I would like to see it."

"It's not in the forest. It's here." Hopefully, Scorpio removed the orb from its pouch and placed it on the table between them.

The old man peered seriously at the object for a few seconds, then began to roar with laughter. "This is a spoiled turnip. Not even good enough for my cooking pot. I had forgotten what a trickster the *Lesovik* was supposed to be." The orb did look flaccid and pitiful; it no longer held even a flicker of its inner light. Scorpio quickly snatched it back and held it against himself, as if to protect it from Igor's ridicule.

In her travels with Scorpio, sometimes Leah had found his emotions unfathomable, but the look of loss on his face was now easy for her to see. The orb was dead. He would have to give it up, Leah thought, and along with it all his dreams and plans of helping his people. It would be hard, and this place was not promising, but they would have to learn to live here.

"Very well," said Igor. "You're too weary to explain anything to me now. I've lived many years and seen many strange things. One learns patience. You'll feel better after a night's sleep. Come, your sleeping accommodations are in the loft above."

Igor lit an oil lamp and led the way up a crude ladder fastened to the wall. Hangings of leather divided the loft into two rooms, and a straw pallet lay in each. Several baskets of corn and barley and a side of salt pork and haunch of smoked beef suspended from the rafters indicated the rooms' usual use. A pile of unused crockery and baskets gathered dust in a corner.

Leah could hear wind whistling through cracks in the log walls, but thick piles of furs on the beds kept the cold at bay. She listened to the sounds of the wind and snuggled deep within the soft coverlets. *This is a primitive world,* she thought. *At least I might be able to make a place for myself here among other human beings, but it's going to be hard for Scorpio.*

Scorpio came down the ladder from the loft the next morning with a feeling of unreality. It didn't seem possible that their travels would end here, in this remote hut decorated with the remains of wild animals. He had no sooner reached the ground floor than he saw Igor approaching wide-eyed, an implement of wood and metal in his hands. Scorpio thought it resembled the weapon the Mishkin brothers had used to kill the wolf, though he wasn't sure how it worked.

"Who are you?" shouted the old man. "For that matter, *what* are you, and how did you get into my *izba?"* The old man's white hair tumbled wildly about his lined face as if he had just surprised an intruder.

It took Scorpio a few moments to realize that was just what the old man thought. He ceased breathing for a moment, wondering what would happen when Igor heard Leah begin to descend. By the way the old man clutched the weapon, and his wildly staring eyes, Scorpio was afraid he already knew.

"Diedushka," said Scorpio, speaking gently and using the deferential term of address he'd heard Misha use. "Don't you remember. Yesterday my companion and I arrived here with the Mishkin brothers. You were kind enough to offer us shelter." Patiently, and yet hurriedly, Scorpio went over each detail of their arrival there the day before.

Scorpio thought the old man had begun to calm somewhat when Leah popped quickly through the trapdoor above them with a cheerful greeting. The old man's nerves gave out and the gun went off with a roar. Leah screamed, lost her hold on the ladder and fell like a wounded bird.

"You've killed her!" shouted Scorpio, and launched himself at the old man. For his age, Igor was robust, and larger than Scorpio, but the alien had the advantage of surprise. He wrested the weapon out of the old man's hands. The Aquay were a timid species, but Scorpio knew that he had changed. He felt an almost human anger rising as he thought of Leah lying on the floor behind him. He had no idea of how to use the weapon, but he raised it menacingly as a club.

"Look," said Igor in an unsteady voice. "She's all right."

Scorpio wouldn't look at first, keeping his eyes on Igor. Leah had tried to warn him that human beings often lied. Then he heard Leah's low moan and turned to look. She was groggily sitting up.

Both of them went to her. "What happened?" she asked. "I heard an explosion and—"

Igor looked shaken. "I'm sorry," he said. "I didn't remember you, but now it comes back to me. It happens sometimes that a night's sleep erases the whole of the day's events from my mind. Old memories are so clear that sometimes I can almost relive them, with sights and sounds and tastes." Igor looked ashamed, spreading his hands in a helpless gesture.

Scorpio felt himself trembling as his anger ebbed. He realized he was still holding Igor's weapon. It looked old, the metal part of it pitted with rust. When he looked up, he saw that it had still functioned well enough to blast a hole in the beam above.

"Now that we're here we won't let you forget," said Leah. "Every day we can remind you of what you've forgotten."

"You'd do that for me?" asked Igor.

"Of course." Leah looked to Scorpio as if for confirmation of the promise.

"I suppose we might as well, as long as we're here," he said. "But I'm not giving your weapon back. I don't want every day to begin the way this one did."

"A good idea," said Igor. "Come to the kitchen. After all this, we need a big breakfast."

After they had eaten, Leah said, "The brothers called you a healer as well as a shaman. My father was training me to be a doctor."

He looked at her skeptically. "You're young," he said. "Healing is a heavy responsibility. Times have been bad and many in the village are ill. My ways are the old ways. Herbs and other bits of lore. I do what I can, but—" He spread his big hands in a helpless gesture. "Would you like to see my pharmacy?"

"Yes, my father was very wise in the use of plants as medicines, and I'd be glad to hear about your methods."

Igor conducted Leah to a smaller room, the walls of which were lined with shelves filled with containers of all sizes and shapes and materials. "Tarragon," said Igor, reaching far over his head to bring down a ceramic bottle. "Also called the little dragon." Evidently he remembered the place of each medicine on the crowded shelves, for nothing was marked.

"We used that as a soporific and a breath sweetener," said Leah. "And also as a chew before taking other medicine, since it dulls the taste."

Igor looked at her suspiciously, then drew down a gray metal canister. "What about chervil?"

"Used to purify the blood in springtime."

"Why, so it is," Igor said with some surprise. "It seems as if your father taught you well."

"There were those who said he should not have tutored me at all," said Leah. "Women were not doctors in my age, I mean, my country."

"That is foolish. It was my grandmother who taught me most of my herbal lore."

"If you'd let me, I'd like to help you here," said Leah. "There may be things we can teach each other."

Igor was silent a long time, and at first she thought she'd insulted him. Then he spoke, "Once, long ago, I was married. My Katerina. There was none like her, and after she died, the heart was not in me to take another wife. Without a child, I had no one to teach the old secrets, and I never found anyone in the village who wanted to learn them. All the young ones yearn to go to Piter, that wicked city. Look what Grigori Yefimovich Rasputin has done for himself, they say. He was a lowly peasant and look at him now. Yes, look at him now." Igor made a disgusted sound. "I'd be glad of your help."

One morning Leah came down from the loft, to see Igor putting on his sheepskin coat. When he looked up, she quickly began to repeat the story, now fixed in her mind like a litany, of how she and Scorpio had come there.

"I remember, I remember," said Igor, laughing.

"Where are you off to?"

"I have to go into the village for some supplies."

"Can I go with you?" asked Leah. She had been curious about the village the Mishkin brothers had talked of.

"I suppose so. You look human enough not to cause concern." His eyes indicated the loft above, where Scorpio still slept. She supposed she shouldn't sneak away without wakening Scorpio, but Igor was right about the effect he was likely to have in the village.

From a shed behind the house Igor led out a stocky pony. With a few well-practiced motions he harnessed the pony and fastened it to the shafts of a small sleigh. "It's only a short distance to Tutalsk," he said, lifting Leah easily up to the seat.

Forest and snow-covered hills went by in a blur. Leah watched alertly as they approached the village, eager to see every detail of the place that would now become her home. A fence surrounded the village, and at the place where it crossed the road stood a gate and gatekeeper's hut. The scene was familiar to Leah. In Avignon walls surrounded the Jewish sector and none could enter or leave from sundown to sunset.

The gatekeeper, muffled in sheepskins, waved cheerfully and opened the gate as Igor's sleigh approached. The village consisted of two long rows of houses built of undressed, unpainted logs caulked with moss, and a tall building with an onion-shaped dome painted a serene blue. Igor, who noticed her gaze, said with pride, "That's our church."

Though rough and plain, the houses had elaborately carved window frames, and some boasted brightly colored shutters. When there was not enough glass to fill the windows, the residents made do with birch bark. The wide street had no sidewalks and there was not a tree or bush in the whole settlement. Bristly, slab-sided pigs trotted at liberty along the street, rooting in the slush in search of food.

Igor pulled back on the reins and stopped the pony in front of the largest structure in the town. "This is the office of

Chernenko, the local fur buyer, but he also keeps a store to provision the villagers and hunters."

As she entered she saw that the walls were of unpainted boards, greasy and stained, and she was hit with a barrage of smells—raw skins, wood smoke, tobacco, spices, everything intermingled in a signature odor of the place. Midway in the large room sat a huge iron stove. Flickers of light dancing around the edges of the doors indicated a fire within. A circle of moujiks, peasants who lived in the village, had pulled up chairs around the stove and were engaged in intent conversation. They were big and rough-looking, with uncut hair and beards, bright-colored shirts under long coats called kaftans, and trousers tucked into high felt boots or leggings made of birch bark.

Igor indicated the squat, swarthy-skinned man behind the counter. "That is Pavel Pyotrovich Chernenko, the fur buyer. And the girl over there dusting shelves is his daughter, Natalia Pavlovna." Leah smiled as Natalia looked at them over her shoulder. *Igor is kind, but it would be nice sometimes to talk to someone more my own age*, Leah thought.

Natalia only gave them a haughty look and turned back to her work. Leah was still wearing the rags of the dress she had come in, under the huge coat that Mikhail had loaned her. *I must look like a ragpicker*, she thought, observing the young woman's costume enviously: on the outside an ordinary apron, below a blue and yellow print skirt held up by two shoulder straps of matching material passing over the loose bodice.

She wandered along the shelves until she saw a display of brightly printed cloth. There's so much of it. And the weave is so fine. It must have taken an army of weavers to make all this.

After a moment she went over to Igor. "Do you think you could buy me some of that cloth, and some needles and thread? If I'm going to be staying here, it might be well if I resembled others in dress. And my cloth shoes and thin stockings won't do in this climate."

"Of course, it was thoughtless of me," said Igor, "but I've lived by myself so long, what do I know about what a girl wants? Get what you need and I'll buy it, along with the things I came after. That coat fits you badly, and you'll need *valenki*, boots of felt. I'm sure Natalia Pavlovna can find everything you need."

After she had made her purchases and was waiting for their parcels to be tied up, Leah walked about the room. Most of the walls were taken up with shelves of merchandise, but the store also had icons such as those in Igor's house. One of them was quite fascinating. Not a picture of a haloed figure, surrounded by candles, it was simply a square wooden box fastened to the wall. A hom like protuberance jutted from the front, and a bracket on the side held another bell-shaped object. On the opposite side was a piece of bent metal like a handle or a crank.

She assumed that it had to be an object of some religious significance like the other things hung upon the walls. Just as they were ready to go, she saw Chernenko go up to the device and turn the crank of it rapidly. The bell device was held to one ear and she saw him talking quietly into the hom. She decided this must be some sort of ritual, an odd form of worship, but she didn't ask Igor about it because she feared offending him.

A few days later Leah was at the edge of the woods gathering lichen for use in poultices. The day was clear and almost mild, sunlight glittering off the snow. She was dawdling, enjoying the sun's warmth, when she saw something in the distance, moving across the snowscape. As it came nearer, she saw that it was a convoy of slow-moving sledges. Behind it trailed a line of raggedly dressed people. She could see that they were chained together.

Something about that grim procession frightened her, the cursing drivers whipping their floundering horses, the silently trudging captives, men and women, their eyes cast down as if all hope was now beyond them. Before she could be seen, she stepped back into the shadow of trees and thickets. When she emerged, sledges and captives were dwindling in the distance, then they went behind a line of trees and were gone.

Leah shivered and, her basket only half full, returned to the *izba.* "You're coming back so soon," remarked Igor. "Did you get cold? You look pale."

"I saw something passing by. Perhaps you can explain it." When she described what she had seen, Igor was silent, watching a curl of smoke rise from his pipe.

"Those unfortunates are bound for a prison camp farther north," said Igor. "You and I know that Siberia is a beautiful place, even though the climate is sometimes a bit harsh, but the Tsar uses it as a place of exile for those who speak out against him."

"Those people were imprisoned because of something they said?" Leah asked. "By the punishment, I would have thought they were all murderers or felons."

"The tsars have held sway over us for generations with their Cossack troops and their *knouts.* Out here we are simple folk, and that sort of justice made sense, but—" He shook his head. "I am told that a new age is coming to Russia. I am too old for a new age. I hope I don't live to see it." With that he fell silent, sucking on the stem of his pipe and staring into space, as he did sometimes, probably lost in his memories.

Still thinking about the unhappy convoy, Leah went into the kitchen. There she found Scorpio sitting near the oven turning the orb over and over in his hands with a hopeless look.

She began telling him about what she had seen, then stopped because it was obvious he wasn't paying any attention. "That isn't going to help, you know," she said at last.

"What isn't?"

"Staring at the orb as if willing it to revive. It should be obvious by now that it's not going to come back to life."

"That would mean my mission is at an end. I can't return to my own world and rescue my people from the Hunters. No, that won't do at all. I won't hear of it!"

Leah saw that the mere presence of the orb was false hope. *I have to get it away from him. Put it away where he won't see it every day. We can make a life for ourselves here. I've got to show him that.* She quickly reached out and tried to take the small globe from his grasp, but he hung on and for a moment they fought for control of it.

Leah thought she felt a tingle as their hands came together. Scorpio looked at her as if he had felt something too, and hope began to dawn on his face. A flicker of wan greenish light slipped between their fingers. Flickered and failed and flickered again.

Scorpio shouted, "It's recovering!"

Igor rushed into the room. Scorpio held up the orb, almost incoherent from joy. "Look, it's alive!"

Igor stared in amazement as pale light formed a hazy nimbus around the orb.

"By the saints, you *are* magical," he said with awe. "What can it do? Show me!"

"No, it's only just recovering," said Scorpio. "I can't ask anything of it now. It needs rest and warmth."

Leah looked on, feeling vaguely unsettled. How quickly she had made plans for a life that really didn't include Scorpio. She wondered if she weren't beginning to weary of adventures with the strange being—if she didn't really hunger for a life more in keeping with human desires.

"This means we're not stranded here after all," Scorpio told her. "If this place doesn't suit us, we'll soon be able to move on to another, until we find someone who can help me control the orb."

Leah wondered briefly if she wouldn't have been happier to have the orb dead. Pushing the thought aside, she tried to look cheerful for Scorpio's sake. After all, she had decided to come with him of her own free will, and she didn't think he'd stop her if she was able at some point to make a place among her own kind. "I'm sure we'll find someone who can help," she said.

The next day Leah was busy sweeping the debris of ages out of Igor's pharmacy when she heard shouts from outside. She had hardly reached the door when a woman burst in, carrying a blanket-wrapped bundle in her arms.

Igor ran in from another room and asked, "Varvara Maximovna, what's the matter?"

The woman looked desperate. Her sides heaved and her cheeks were burned a dull red from the bite of the wind.

"It's my Nikki," she said, pulling back the edge of the blanket to expose the flushed face of a child about three years old.

Igor took the child from her gently and carried him into the pharmacy where he laid him on a small cot bed in the corner. Leah watched carefully as Igor examined the child. "He's burning with fever," said Igor, inviting Leah to lay her hand on the child's dry, hot flesh.

"He was fine last night, playing by the hearth," said Varvara. "Then this morning—" She began to sob.

"Help me to get snow," Igor said to Leah. "Sometimes a fever can be brought down that way."

Overhearing them, Scorpio came to help as they scooped snow into whatever kitchen vessel they could lay hands on. Carefully they packed the snow around the boy's small body. When it melted, sending rivulets along the dusty floorboards, Igor ordered them to get more. After a while Leah could no longer feel her hands, but she stayed at the task anyway. At intervals Igor touched the boy's head and limbs to see if the fever had gone down.

Leah had just returned with another full pail of snow when Igor looked up at her, shaking his head. "No. No more. It's not working."

"But what about your pharmacy?" asked Scorpio. "Isn't there something—"

Leah touched the child's cheek. "Sometimes, for all our remedies, there's nothing we can do. We just don't know enough."

"We could use the orb," said Scorpio. Leah looked at him in surprise. The orb had earlier shown the powers of healing and it had helped her to recover from the loss of her family, but for all its magic, even the orb had its limits.

"If we use it too soon and drain its powers, it may not recover again," said Leah. "Are you sure?"

"If he's dying," said Scorpio, "we have to take the chance."

Scorpio hurried to get the orb. By the time he brought it back, the boy was struggling to breathe. Air rasped in his throat, a harsh, ugly sound. Gently Scorpio placed the orb on the boy's chest where it began to pulse with light in rhythm to the boy's ragged breathing. Scorpio looked worried, afraid that the light would again go out, but though the radiance dimmed, it cast a steady glow.

The child's face now seemed more composed, and the hectic flush of his cheeks began to pale. His breathing grew deeper and quieter. Leah touched the boy's skin and found it cool.

When she turned around, she saw Nikki's mother on her knees in an attitude of prayer, her eyes turned up to Scorpio and the orb as if she knew she was witnessing a miracle. Leah briefly wished that Igor had taken her into the other room, but then Varvara came to take the child into her arms, and Leah relented. Still, it didn't seem a good idea for her to have seen both Scorpio and the powers of the orb.

"He's all right," Varvara whispered.

"Yes, and so is the orb," said Scorpio. Its light still shone, though it was paler.

It would probably have been too much to hope that the woman would remain silent after witnessing a miracle. The village was soon buzzing with the news. Vasily heard women gossiping about it in the store and quickly returned home.

"It's all over town," Vasha told his brother. "A strange gray man who healed a child by magic. *Our* gray man. Igor tricked us into leaving him."

"I thought you left the creatures there for safekeeping," said Misha.

"It seemed a good idea at the time," said Vasha, "but how was I to know the *Lesovik* had the healing touch? You know of our countryman Grigori Rasputin, and how he has become physician to the Tsar's ailing son? And how influential he has become at court?"

"Everyone knows of that. It is old news," said Misha.

"How many times have we said we could shake the dust of this town from our feet if only there was some way? The gray man is our way."

"Of course," said Misha, his round, red-cheeked face lighting up and the characteristic gap-toothed smile appearing. "We will go to Igor's and claim him right now."

"Well ... perhaps that isn't such a good idea."

"Why not? He has what is ours."

"Being a healer, Igor probably knows how valuable the *Lesovik* is. He might say that the *Lesovik* has a right to decide where he wishes to live. No, this calls for cleverness, and stealth. Do not strain yourself, brother. Leave it to me. I will come up with a plan."

Chapter Three

Leah drove Igor's sturdy pony at a brisk trot along the road to the village. After the miraculous cure of little Nikki, Igor had begun to show more confidence in her. This place wasn't so bad, after all, she told herself as the runners sang along the hard-packed road and the bracing wind made her cheeks tingle. It had become a little wearisome introducing themselves to Igor each morning, but his memory did seem to be improving a little, and Scorpio had returned his rifle. It might have been her chance to use the healing skills her father had taught her, but now Scorpio talked of nothing but jumping again to some more advanced time. She had to share in his happiness that the powers of the orb weren't gone forever; a friend could do no less. But she had only just begun to make a place for herself here.

When she reached the store, she saw that for once the chairs beside the stove were empty. Silence seemed strange. She missed the usual discussion and cheerful arguments of the moujiks.

Natalia Pavlovna seemed happy to see Leah, but this was odd because the girl had always kept quite aloof, as though thinking herself the superior because of her father's position in the village.

"May I beg a favor of you," Natalia said. "The seamstress is finishing a dress for me and she wanted me to try it on this morning. Business is slow, as you see, and I'd be back in a few minutes. Could you watch the store until I return?"

Leah agreed, and Natalia left happily. The store was to Leah a fascinating place—food in tins with pictures of what was inside embossed into the lids, bolts of cloth of such fine weave she wasn't sure how they could have been made on the hand looms she was used to.

When she had asked Natalia about it, the other girl had only said curtly that it had been made in a factory, with the air that only someone extremely ignorant wouldn't know what a factory was. When she had asked Igor about it, he said that he thought he had once visited a factory, but wasn't sure because he had forgotten.

With the material and a sewing kit Igor had bought, Leah had made a full-skirted dress in the style the peasant girls wore.

Now, as she stood waiting for Natalia to return, the icon she had noticed on the wall earlier began to make a jangling noise. She had seen it do this numerous times. Sometimes, everyone in the room ignored it, but sometimes Chernenko or one of the idlers would rush to the icon and, holding the bell up to his ear, would speak into the horn, exactly as if they thought that by so doing they could contact whatever god they worshiped. Leah was fascinated by this, but as yet hadn't said anything to Igor for fear that he too believed in the god of the wooden icon.

As the icon continued to jangle, Leah had a sudden urge to step up to it as Chernenko had. If others had been in the room, she never would have done so, fearing to seem blasphemous, but curiosity drew her. Impulsively she lifted the bell to her ear.

"Hello, is this Chernenko?" said a stern voice.

Leah nearly dropped the bell from surprise.

"Chernenko, are you there?"

Leah stood petrified, even though after the first few seconds had passed, she had realized that this was the voice of an ordinary man, though it had a peculiar hollow quality ringing out against a hissing background noise.

Quickly she put the bell back into its cradle, just as Natalia came back in.

"It doesn't seem as if you were busy in my absence," said Natalia. "It only took a few minutes. Father need never know. Leah, aren't you listening. You look so pale."

Leah indicated the phone and the wall behind it. "Is this a trick? Does someone hide in a secret closet and speak through that box?"

"My, you are ignorant," said Natalia smugly. "The voice of someone speaking far away is carried by a wire— or at least I think that's right. Anyway, it's just a simple telephone, though of course no one else in the village has one except Father. But you haven't been meddling with it, have you?"

"Oh, no," Leah assured her. "I'm just ignorant, as you say."

She still felt stunned, wondering whether she should believe a person's words could be carried long distances over a wire and come out through this box. If Natalia was joking, and she didn't seem the type for humor, then this time was more advanced than they had believed. She had to return quickly to tell Scorpio the good news.

She told Natalia what she needed, drumming her fingertips on the countertop as the girl moved here and there, collecting her order. *Why does she have to be so slow?*Leah wondered.

She rushed outside and threw the parcels into the sleigh. The horse caught her mood of anxiety, moving out before she had brought down the reins on his back. Scorpio will be so pleased. I can't wait to get back and tell him, she thought. She suddenly realized that her eagerness to get back had so taken possession of her that she had urged the pony to his fastest pace. Like a runaway he careened along the icy ruts of the road, but she made no move to slow him.

A feeling of foreboding, like a low-hanging cloud, began to invade her mind. There must be a more urgent reason to return to the *izba*, even if she was certain what it was. *Danger to Scorpio?* she wondered. Her mental connection to the alien had atrophied during the orb's weakness, but now that the orb was growing stronger, it might be returning. If so, all was not well in the *izba* of Igor Dmitrovitch.

Vasha and Misha approached the *izba* cautiously; it was the only way to approach Igor since he would often mistake acquaintances for marauding strangers. Though his memory was going fast, there was nothing wrong with his shooting. "Ho, *Diedushka*!" shouted Misha. "It is we—the brothers Mishkin. We have come to see how the *Lesovik* fares!"

The door opened a crack, and the beaked face of the creature appeared. "Igor isn't here. Someone came to get him, saying his father was ill and couldn't be moved."

"What luck," said Misha in a whisper. Vasha gave him a quelling look.

"That is an unhappy coincidence because we bring news. Your young woman companion has met with an accident in the village. Her sleigh overturned." Vasha had seen Leah arrive in the village; otherwise he would have concocted some other story.

The door swung inward to admit the brothers. Anxiety about his friend made the *Lesovik* careless. Vasha had counted on that.

"Leah did take the sleigh into the village this morning," said Scorpio.

"She has been calling for you," said Misha. "We came straightaway to take you to her."

"That was kind," said Scorpio, but the words seemed to cover a wariness. "Leah is injured, you say."

"Yes, a terrible accident," said Vasha.

There was a silence as Scorpio seemed in some manner to go within himself, as if somewhere inside his mind he might find evidence of their lie.

Vasha pushed that thought aside. If the lie was plausible enough, it would be believed. Even if this creature was a *Lesovik* or other supernatural being, which Vasha had doubted from the first, there was no way he could know what happened in the village.

"I believe she is on her way back now," said Scorpio. "I can see the bobbing bay rump of Igor's pony, feel the rocking of the sleigh. Perhaps you aren't telling the truth." He looked at them with his staring alien eyes, and Misha began to scuff his feet nervously on the boards of the floor. "What reason would you have to lie?"

Their scheme ruined, Vasha leapt forward and caught the alien in a bear hug. Scorpio was slender, so Vasha had no doubt he could hold on to him easily.

"Get the bag we brought along in the sleigh," he told Misha, who hurried away.

"What do you want with me?" gasped Scorpio.

"You forget that we found you in the first place. We have come to claim our property." Vasha suddenly doubled over in pain as Scorpio's elbow caught him in the stomach. The creature managed to break free, but as he ran for the door, Misha returned. "Be careful," warned Vasha, "he's stronger than he looks. Tricky, too."

Vasha grabbed Scorpio from behind and Misha flopped the heavy bag over his head and arms and secured it with a rope. As Vasha lifted Scorpio off his feet to carry him to the sleigh, he felt a snap. The being's struggles had broken the thongs that attached a fur pouch to his belt. "What's that?" asked Misha as the pouch rolled across the floor.

"It's nothing," said Vasha. "Let's get out of here before Igor Dmitrovitch returns."

"He's a great deal of trouble," said Misha as they loaded Scorpio into the sleigh. "I hope we'll be able to control him after we get to Petrograd."

"He'll do what we say, or else," said Vasha. "After all, he's ours by right. We're the ones who found him."

"What about the girl?"

"What about her? She's of no value to us. This creature is the one who healed Nikki. Didn't his mother witness it?"

"You don't think the girl will find a way to come after us?"

"What if she does? Are you frightened of a mere girl?

"Be silent!" he shouted at Scorpio who was still struggling, his cries muffled by the thick cloth of the sack.

"Maybe he's trying to tell us he's suffocating in there," said Misha.

"Get him some air, then, onion head," said Vasha. "He is of no use to us dead."

Misha used his skinning knife to cut a hole in the top of the bag. Scorpio's head appeared. For a moment the being gasped for air.

"Where are you taking me?" Scorpio asked, still coughing from the grain dust in the bottom of the sack.

"Piter," said Vasha. "It's a vast city. I was there once. You'll like it. A healer such as yourself will create a great sensation."

"Don't be so certain that I'm a healer," said Scorpio.

"No use in being modest," said Vasha. "Everyone in the village knows."

"How are we going to get him on the train, brother?" asked Misha. "There'll be a riot when people see him. And what of a passport?"

"I have thought of everything," said Vasha. "I brought a fur hat and a muffler to cover his head and face, and I have borrowed the passport of Uncle Vlad."

"But he's been dead for ten years."

"Then he won't come looking for it, will he?"

"Oh."

Leah pulled up the lathered pony before the *izba*, feeling foolish. She couldn't be sure that the anxiety she had felt really meant anything. Everything looked peaceful, just as it had when she had left that morning. She hurried inside calling first Scorpio's name, then Igor's. No one answered.

Maybe they went out on a medical emergency, she told herself, trying to remain calm. She went back outside and unharnessed the pony, rubbed him down and put him in the shed with a reward of grain. By the time she returned to the *izba*, Igor was there.

"Do you know where Scorpio has gone?" she asked.

"No, he was here when I left, but maybe he went out for some reason."

"Where would he go?"

As she crossed the room, she caught sight of something in a corner. When she knelt to retrieve it, she saw that it was the fur bag Scorpio used to carry the orb. She opened it and a ray of golden light emerged. She noticed the thongs of the bag were broken. "He wouldn't leave without this," she said. "I knew it! Something terrible must have happened to him!"

"I'm sure all is well," said Igor, "but maybe we should look around outside."

As they left the *izba* they soon came upon two sets of tracks, one pressed deeply into the snow as if a man had been carrying something heavy. The trail led to a screen of foliage, and from there to the parallel track of sleigh runners.

Leah followed the trail for a short distance, until she grew tired enough to let Igor convince her to return home.

"Why would anyone want to do Scorpio harm?" she asked later as she sat wrapped in a blanket atop Igor's oven, trying to stop shivering. "We didn't even allow him to go into the village, so most people didn't even know he existed."

Igor stroked his white beard. "Of course, Varvara considered Nikki's cure a miracle. She could not have kept such news to herself. And we can't forget the brothers Mishkin. Vasily made sure I knew he considered the two of you his property. But no, they are loafers and ne'er-do-wells, not brigands. They would never hurt anyone. Perhaps a wandering band of robbers—"

Leah looked alarmed. Igor fell silent.

The whooping of the wind outside reminded them that snow would quickly be blown over the tracks of the sleigh. There was still one possibility, Leah decided: the telepathic bond she and Scorpio had developed. It had waned when the orb became dormant, but she had felt vague stirrings of its return. Now she let the warmth of the coals relax her and tried to attune herself to Scorpio.

Details of the landscape flew by in a darkening blur. After his first panic about being tied up and carried off, Scorpio began to regain a little confidence. As he listened to the brothers talk, he realized that they had plans of their own in which he seemed to figure importantly. When he complained of the tightness of the ropes, Misha had obligingly loosened them. They didn't seem to intend him any real harm, so he was no longer so afraid. From what he overheard, their plans had something to do with his abilities as a healer. He didn't think it was a good idea to let them know just now that without the orb his healing powers were nil; they would be unlikely to believe him, anyway. It would sound as if he were lying so they would release him.

For the moment there was little he could do except to try to get a message through to Leah about where the brothers were taking him. The level of concentration needed for contact was almost painful. He knew that the telepathic bond between himself and Leah had been broken when the orb's light was lost, but it had begun to return. The mind-link had returned to him more readily than it had to Leah, possibly because she had been so busy establishing herself among her own kind.

He hadn't taken a similar interest in those around him because superstitious as they were, the village folk would always look on him with something akin to terror. Being carried off and held captive wouldn't have been his choice of a way to depart the village, but he didn't mind leaving it.

If he could only get his message through to Leah, he was sure she would find a way to follow, bringing the orb. He put all his energy into letting her know their destination: Piter, Petrograd.

Leah awoke with a start, realizing that Igor had forgone his oven sleeping place for one night because she had fallen asleep there. The surface beneath her was hard and cold; the coals had all gone out during the night. But swimming up through layers of dream, she had not surfaced empty-handed. A word had shaped itself in her consciousness.

Igor had just tiptoed in. He looked startled when she sat up, and she explained who she was and how she had gotten there for the nth time. Igor was nodding contentedly when she finished. "How could I do without you," he smiled. "You're my memory."

"Sometime in the night I came up with a word: Piter. Do you know it?"

"Of course. Everyone knows that. It's a large city hundreds of versts from here. It's where the Tsar holds court. Though I don't remember offhand who the Tsar is just now ... Is it Alexander ... Nicholas?"

"That doesn't matter. If it's a place, it's the place Scorpio is being taken. How can I get there?"

"You'd go running off across the country because of a dream you had?"

"It isn't exactly a dream. Since I hadn't heard the word before, it must have come through to me from Scorpio."

Igor looked at her in awe. "Even though you look human, you are as strange as he is," he said.

Leah wasn't sure she liked the sound of that, but Scorpio was helpless without the orb. Though she had been an orb-traveler, Scorpio had been the one to maintain whatever tenuous control they had over it. She didn't dare try to use it without him.

"How can I get to this city?" she asked again.

"Well, I suppose I could take you to the station at Irkutsk in my sleigh, and you could take the train from there. But it's a huge and wicked city."

"I know something of cities," she said, remembering Avignon and later London.

"All right, since I see I cannot dissuade you."

That afternoon Igor drove Leah up before the station. She felt none of the confidence she had tried to show him earlier. She didn't even know what it meant to "take a train," and she didn't want to ask because Igor mentioned it so casually, as if everyone should know.

"Well, I suppose I must say goodbye," she said, alighting from the sleigh.

"Wait," he said. He handed a paper-wrapped parcel down to her. "Varvara gave me this, in gratitude for saving the boy's life. It's her life's savings—not much, I suppose, but it should be useful to you. I need no money in Tutalsk."

"Igor, you've been a good friend," said Leah, honestly sorry now to be leaving.

"I don't understand why you must go," he said, "but since you must, go with my blessing."

She watched as he turned the horse about and started away.

"Remember me!" she shouted, but Igor was already an insubstantial figure behind a curtain of windblown snow.

The station was filled to capacity with people, staid moujiks and their *babas.* Children tugging at parents' hands or grasping a mother's skirt. Uniformed soldiers gathering around the boiling samovar to make tea or loitering in the doorways chewing and spitting out sunflower seeds. There was also a sprinkling of well-to-do kulaks and merchants, flaunting their fine clothes.

As at the fur buyer's store, the men were continually talking, arguing, debating the latest events. Leah had begun to believe that in Russia debate was some sort of national pastime. "I've come to take the train to Piter," she said to a plump peasant woman, hoping it wasn't obvious that she didn't know what a train was. In a bored manner, the woman directed her toward a barred window set into the wall.

She repeated her request, and the man behind the bars produced a slip of paper. Leah opened the packet Igor had given her, the coin and the word *ruble* joining neatly in her mind so that she was able to count out the amount of money it took to buy her fare. She began to feel that Igor might have been right about her journey. She had hardly begun it and she felt lost already.

She waited for what seemed a long time. At last she turned to a well-dressed old man with a kindly look. "I'm taking the train to Piter," she said. "Shouldn't it have arrived by now?"

"Of course. It should have been here twenty minutes ago," said the man with a laugh. "That is the one thing you can depend on these days: the trains never run on time. I hope you're not in a hurry."

After a while she heard a noise, distant at first, rhythmic and powerful. Along with this came a thin wailing, like a cry for help in a mechanical throat. The sound of it unsettled Leah, but she was even more frightened by the metal behemoth that came huffing and snorting right up to the station door. It was black and immense, moving parts clattering together, steam shooting from vents in its sides. The worst thing about it was the uncanny way it moved, but it was not pulled by any horses or oxen that she could see.

She didn't want to go a step nearer the thing, but the surging crowd pushed her out onto the platform. The black beast had gone by but it pulled a tail of rumbling metal carriages. When the carriage doors opened, the crowd stampeded. Leah found herself pummeled, pushed and carried along by the momentum of the crowd. Rather than be trampled, she jumped up and through one of these open doors.

Once inside she looked around wildly. Seats ran along both sides of the narrow carriage with tiny windows by each seat. Many of the seats were already filled and people were pushing around her and taking their places. Seeing an empty seat, she scuttled forward, falling into it as the train snorted and jerked forward.

"Aiii, we're moving!" she shrieked, as she saw the landscape begin to move slowly past the windows. The soldier sleeping in the seat beside her wakened, and he stared at her with heavy-lidded eyes.

"Did you expect to reach our destination with the train standing still?" he asked. He had a stocky body and a round, placid peasant's face. There was something wrong with his face and his voice, too, Leah realized, but she was too terrified to figure out what it was just now. "I know that the trains never run on time as it is, but at least one has hope if it moves at all."

Leah gripped the edges of the seat as the train reached what she considered an incredible speed. "Human beings weren't meant to go this fast," she said. "Won't it do something to you?"

"You must really be from the backcountry if you've never ridden a train before," said the soldier good-humoredly. "I come from Siberia myself. But I'd almost think you'd never *seen* a train before. Here, have some bread and cheese and calm down." He reached into a basket on the floor beside Leah and brought out the food wrapped in a napkin. As he opened it on the seat between them, Leah saw that the soldier had small, graceful hands. A woman's hands.

She stared at the soldier's face again. That was what it was: no beard, full lips and a voice higher in pitch than it should have been. Before speaking she looked again at the bulky uniform, creased and stained, the well-oiled rifle leaning against the seat. These looked as if they'd seen hard use. They weren't part of a costume in some strange masquerade. Was this soldier a man or woman? Leah longed to ask, but knew she would sound like an idiot if she was wrong.

"My mother prepared enough for ten—what's wrong? Why are you staring?"

"You're a woman!" Leah blurted out, unable to stop herself.

"You observe closely; many people don't notice."

"But you're a soldier."

"Correct again. Maria Leontievna Botchkareva of the Polotsk regiment, at your service."

Leah was stunned into silence. Voices in the close-packed car mingled with the rhythmic *clackety-clack* of the wheels over the rails. "Women aren't soldiers," said Leah at last.

Botchkareva was amused by this strange backcountry girl who was surprised by everything. "So everyone kept trying to tell me," she said, remembering how she was laughed at when she had first attempted to enlist. "Only by writing a letter to the Tsar and receiving a special dispensation was I allowed to become a soldier."

She would never know why the Tsar gave his permission, though she supposed he had his reasons. He was a great patriot and even now had gone to the front to command the troops.

Her own reasons were a little vague, when she looked back on it. She always told people that she had enlisted because her husband had been killed in the war, but that wasn't true. He had been a good husband at first, but he became a professional gambler and his attitude changed. He became so violent she decided she could no longer live with him. Her parents had always lived in poverty, so she couldn't run to them. But even in northern Siberia tales were told about the war, and the idea of enlisting in the army took hold of her imagination.

"You really went through military training, lived among only men?" asked Leah.

"In the barracks that first night I hardly got a wink of sleep. The men supposed I was a woman of loose morals, joining the ranks only to carry on her illicit trade. I had only my fists to prove them wrong, but once I had convinced them of my motives, many of them accepted me. They gave me the nickname Yashka."

"At the front, my commanding officer at first refused to let me fight. 'Women weren't made for war,' he told me, but when I passed a thorough test of what I had learned in training, he was forced to give me a chance."

"Weren't you afraid?"

Botchkareva nodded. "I remember my first battle. The commander had ordered us to put on our gas masks. The masks weren't perfect, so some of the gas leaked through, making my eyes smart and water. Then our commander cried, *'Viliezai,'* 'Climb out.' I felt half-paralyzed, wondering why I had ever decided this was something I could do, but the boys were climbing out of the trenches and I couldn't let them see how afraid I was, not after I'd tried so hard to convince them that I was one of them, another soldier. I felt as if I had stepped into hell, machine-gun fire raking the ground before me and cutting down soldiers like ripe wheat harvested by a huge invisible scythe.

"When we reached the enemy's barbed-wire entanglements, we saw that their artillery had failed to demolish the barriers. The order was given to retreat. The retreat was worse than the advance. By the time we reached our trenches, there were only forty-eight left alive. About a third of the 250 lay dead. Most of the wounded were in no-man's-land. I could remember them crying out in pain or for someone to help them or to kill them.

"As the hours wore on, I realized I couldn't just stay in the trenches and listen. I climbed out, worming my away across the rugged ground until I reached a soldier. I began to pull him back toward the trenches. Machine-gun fire kicked up dust from the ground nearby and I flopped down, lying still so that they would think I was dead. When a lull in the firing came, I continued dragging him to safety. Seeing one man picked up and carried off by medical personnel gave me the encouragement to go back out again. I was so exhausted I didn't keep track, but by morning I was told I had accounted for fifty lives.

"Everyone was afraid," Botchkareva said, "but I didn't do so badly. I never had to prove to the men again that I was one of them."

"But why are you here? Have you had enough of war?"

"I was wounded three times. The last time I had been too close when a German shell landed. I still carry a fragment of it in my body. The doctors didn't believe that I would ever be able to walk again, but I've recovered almost completely."

She smiled to herself as she remembered the day she went before the military medical commission to be released from the hospital. After a long period of recuperation, she was anxious to leave and feeling mischievous as she was led into a large room where about 200 other patients awaited examination and word whether they would be sent home or considered well enough to be sent back to the front. When the chairman of the commission, a general, read her name, he considered it a mistake and changed it to Marin Botchkarev. *"Razdievaysia!"* shouted the general, the order given to every soldier being examined. "Undress!"

She walked up boldly and threw off her outer garment, and stood in her underwear. A panic ensued, with soldiers laughing and shouting and the medical panel sitting there stunned. "A woman!" cried the general. "Why did you undress?"

"Because you gave the order and since I'm a soldier, I obey orders without question."

"Then obey this; put your clothes back on at once!"

"How about the examination, Excellency?" she asked as she put her clothing back on.

"You're passed," he said.

"I've been visiting my parents in Tomsk and now I'm on my way to Petrograd to be awarded the gold cross," Botchkareva continued. "After that, it's back to my regiment. They need me there. Morale has gotten very low." Botchkareva shot a disgusted look across the aisle where a group of men had congregated and were talking and laughing together. They were filthy and unkempt, wearing ragged army uniforms. By their attitude they might have owned the carriage, shouting obscenities and insults at the other passengers as they did.

"Morale is very low," she said in a whisper. "Problems with transportation of goods to the front demoralize the men. There is never enough food, uniforms, boots, ammunition, and there are rumors that the higher officers collaborate with the Germans. Some soldiers have even deserted. Imagine it, to turn tail and run in Mother Russia's hour of need!" She shook her head.

"I'd like to drive them back to the front," she said, patting the stock of her rifle, "but there are too many. I've seen them clinging to the trains, riding on top when there was no more room inside. Someone even made a sign, 'Soldiers, please do not throw passengers out the window while the train is in motion,' though I suppose it may have been a joke. But we have talked only of me. Why are you going to Petrograd?"

"I have a friend who has gone there before me. I hope to join him there, but I'm afraid I know nothing of the city."

"Yes, it's very different from the backcountry. Because of the war and the hard times, there's a great deal of suspicion. You can't move a step without showing some official your papers or passport."

"I have no papers," said Leah embarrassedly. "Will I be arrested?"

Botchkareva looked at her suspiciously, wondering if Leah were a German spy, since she had no explanation of who she was or where she had come from. No, this young woman appeared too innocent. While she didn't seem exactly to fit the mold of peasant, she didn't seem ever to have seen a train before, let alone have traveled on one. *When I ran away from my husband, I could take little with me*, she thought. *Perhaps the friend she is joining is a lover, and she has left everything behind for his sake.* She felt a surge of sympathy.

"The Tsar's agents will probably be checking our papers when we reach the station, but it's well known that in Russia you can have what you want, if you're willing to pay for it."

"A bribe?" asked Leah too loudly.

"Hush, it's not something one broadcasts to the world, but the bureaucracy being as it is these days ... Do you have money?"

Leah quickly produced the napkin full of rubles and unwrapped it. Botchkareva made a gesture for her to wrap it up quickly again. "Don't let those soldiers see that you have money," she cautioned. "When we reach the station, let me do the talking and have your money at the ready." Botchkareva sighed inaudibly, wondering if this naive girl could survive in Petrograd. She doubted it, but she had too many concerns of her own to become involved.

Though she had thought she would never get used to the extreme speed of the train, in talking to the woman soldier, Leah had forgotten all about the landscape moving crazily past the windows. They had eaten all the bread and cheese, and Botchkareva had shifted her position with a grimace as if her wound still pained her and then stretched her legs out before her, pulled down her cap and had gone back to sleep.

Chapter Four

Lethor the Hunter stood inside the translucent golden sphere of the orb-craft. Snowflakes, whirled by the wind, fell softly against its sides making a faint hissing sound as the warmth inside the ball melted them instantaneously.

"This is nothing but wilderness," said his Beta companion, Ardon, stating the obvious as Betas are wont to do. Lethor gave him a look at once patronizing and affectionate. Ardon had been his Beta from infancy; they had been chemically bonded, to function as a team, according to Hunter tradition. Ardon's strength and placidity complemented Lethor's speed and intelligence. The relationship was one even closer than that of male and mate, for mating came only at certain seasons, but hunting was the all-consuming purpose of the race.

As the walls of the craft dissipated, the orb shrank down to fit into Lethor's hand. Then the two Hunters stepped out into the snow, their thick-soled, two-toed feet leaving alien tracks that the wind would soon scour away.

Snowflakes falling on Lethor's face and hands and the snow melting around his ankles made him curse under his breath. A desert-dweller, moisture made his hard red skin burn and crack. Ardon was now feeling the effects, too, and began to move about with discomfort.

Lethor's near-vision brought distant objects into close focus as he looked around. He saw a narrow cave entrance before which two gray-furred beasts rolled and tussled. Near-vision was an inborn reflex in Hunters, but he could call it up at will by concentration. There really wasn't anything else to see, though anxiety made him imagine two small fleeing figures among the close-grown trees of the taiga.

When he had first taken his Hunter's oath to eliminate Scorpio, he had considered the task almost beneath him. The Aquay were timid creatures, who gave little sport to a chase. But ever since Scorpio had stolen an orb and gone careening through time with that blasted female indigene, he had become more than satisfied with the challenge. Lethor loved challenges, but the hunt had gone on a little long and he was anxious to see his home-world again. According to his Hunter's oath, he could not return while Scorpio still lived. Lethor's orb could follow the one Scorpio had, especially if it was being used, though it couldn't pinpoint the exact location.

"Strange," said Lethor, "the orb tells me that the trail ends here."

"Doesn't that thing look a little funny?"

The globe in Lethor's hand had begun to pulse, its golden light turning greenish.

"Nonsense. It's fine. Quickly, back into our craft. We'll try to pick up the trail somehow." Neither of them noticed that before the skin of the orb bubble formed around them, there was a slight flutter, a hesitation.

Igor was in his pharmacy mixing up a philter for a lovesick peasant girl when he thought he heard a noise in the other room. His rifle leaned against one wall at the ready, so he picked it up as he went to investigate. He surprised two hulking intruders, very strange-looking creatures with red skins and beaklike faces and growths like ram's horns curling to either side of their heads. Despite their oddness, there was something familiar about those faces ... and something about this situation reminiscent of some past happening, though he didn't remember what it was.

"Thieves, robbers!" he shouted, putting the gun up to his shoulder and squeezing the trigger.

The gun went off with a roar inside the small hut, but missed both of the intruders and blasted a hole in the wall. The surprise of it and the noise made one of them stagger back, and the other fell down.

Igor took aim again.

One of the creatures raised a hand. A beam of light shot out from a device attached to its wrist, touching Igor's weapon and sizzling along the barrel. With a cry of pain, Igor dropped the suddenly red-hot gun and bolted for the door. Before he'd taken five steps, one of the creatures grabbed him and held him back.

"We seek a gray-skinned being who looks a little like us," said the humming voice. "He is traveling with a human female."

The alien's hands were like bands of metal on Igor's arms. The frightening face approached close to his.

In fear, Igor spoke, "I'm an old man." His voice was weak and quavering. "I live alone here. Only a few people from the village still seek me out for my cures. I have seen nothing like what you describe. If I had I'd certainly remember it, wouldn't I?"

"Are you sure, old man?" The other alien lifted the wrist weapon, aiming it toward Igor's face. Igor remembered the blast of heat that had made his gun too hot to hold, and trembled, then he saw the being's eyes glitter, as if a membrane or lens had briefly flickered over the eyes' surface and was as quickly withdrawn. He actually felt himself under minute scrutiny, as though by some means the being could judge whether or not he was lying.

"Yes, I see that he is telling us the truth. He hasn't seen them. We must seek elsewhere."

Slowly, as if grudgingly, the larger being let Igor sink to the floor. Igor hid his face in his hands, so he didn't see where the creatures went. But when he had composed himself, they were gone.

When he picked up his gun he saw that the barrel was fused, and blackened as if it had been in a furnace.

Later, when he went outside to chop wood, he noticed that storm clouds were looming threateningly in the sky in the direction of Petrograd. That seemed to trigger a memory. When he thought back over it and considered whether or not he had actually seen a gray-skinned creature and a woman companion, he wasn't so sure. It almost seemed as if there was a memory there. The memory of friends.

He shook his head. Things were at a bad pass when the best thing one could do for his friends was to forget them entirely. Before he had finished his wood-chopping chores, he was hearing the music of a festival that had been held over seventy years ago. In his mind's eye he saw his Katerina dancing in a circle with other peasant maidens. He felt the anticipation, as if he were really sixteen again and just about to meet the only woman he had ever loved.

The Hunters' bubble-craft next appeared inside one of the village's crude structures. A group of indigenes that had been gathered around a primitive heating device fell out of their chairs with shouts of surprise and then hastily fled.

Lethor investigated a pile of garments made of the skins of animals. "Here, these will protect us if cold liquid falls from the sky again."

With some clumsiness, the aliens outfitted themselves.

"I think we should have used our weapons on the first indigene," said Ardon.

"He was nothing," said Lethor. "An old fool with an antique projectile weapon. He was not honorable prey."

"Even though it was an antique," said Ardon in his deliberate way, "I think one of us could have been dead all the same. Hunting is an old game to us, but it is played for keeps."

Lethor laughed; a human being would have heard a harsh, vibrating sound. "Indeed it is, old companion. But that old man could do us no harm. Also, as he spoke, I inspected him closely with my near-vision. There are certain ways an intelligent being reacts when telling a falsehood, and I have studied these beings enough to detect them. He had never seen them, so we must continue our search."

When Scorpio saw the train, his spirits rose. He had thought of this world as impossibly backward, but while this conveyance was ugly and noisy, it did go under its own power, suggesting a developing technology. He didn't like the idea of being separated from Leah and the orb, but there wasn't anything he could do about that just now.

"Since the train is moving and I'd be crazy to jump off of it, do you think you could remove these ropes?" Scorpio asked. He was jammed between the two bulky brothers on one seat.

"What do you think, brother?" asked Misha.

"I suppose it would be all right," said Vasha, "but remember, we mean to keep a careful eye on you."

"I doubt if I'd have much chance to get away from the two of you," said Scorpio as Misha reached under the coat to undo the knots. "And I suppose I really should thank you. I was getting weary of staying with that old man. He forced me and my companion to do all the work about the place, as if we were his slaves. And his memory was terrible; we had to spend hours explaining things to the old tyrant."

"Igor's infirmity has become well known about the village," said Misha.

"I used to wish that there was some way to escape from him, and then you two came along. I was startled at first, but then I heard you talking about how you're going to the city to make your fortunes, and that interested me."

"We might have said something of the sort," said Vasha.

"Well, I'm willing to help you. I'm sure there'll be lots of opportunities in the city for clever people like us."

"You'll do all right," said Vasha, "as long as you do what we tell you."

"And if you can really heal the sick as was rumored in the village," added Misha.

"Also, you must be sure to keep your face covered with your muffler. It's cold this time of year and no one will be suspicious."

Scorpio fell silent and began to concentrate again on getting his message through to Leah.

It was late afternoon when the train arrived at Petrograd. The brothers and Scorpio had to stand in a line to show their papers to the officials. Squinting down at the very bad passport photo, the agent looked curiously at Scorpio who had his muffler wrapped around his face with only a slit to look through. "He's sick," said Vasha quickly. Scorpio began to make coughing noises, and the agent looked at him with alarm. There were also a lot of people waiting, so he waved them on through.

At the station they took a horse-drawn cab called a droshky across the city. Scorpio observed the wide squares and prospects laid out with planned perfection along canals, now dark and frozen in the dwindling light. Misha and Vasha prattled like tourists, and he learned that Petrograd had been built under the rule of Peter the Great. Thousands of serfs had worked and died so that a city could rise on what had once been a swamp.

They drove past structures with onion-shaped domes, tiled in blue and gold, and massive and ornate buildings topped with statuary. Ornate grille fences were everywhere, iron and bronze lacework, black and gilded.

As they passed the wider expanse of the frozen river called the Neva, he saw on the opposite bank a slender spire shining like a needle of gold. "That is beautiful," said Scorpio. "What is it?"

"Beautiful, he says," laughed Vasha. "Not so beautiful for them inside. The Saints Peter and Paul Fortress is a prison where the tsars put their enemies, for safekeeping, you might say." He laughed. "So safe nobody ever sees them again."

They drove past a structure the brothers called the Winter Palace. Its facade was pale green, with many windows and immense marble columns. When he commented upon how this building dominated the skyline, the brothers laughed and said that the tsars had insured that by passing an edict that prohibited building anything taller than the Winter Palace.

They passed countless monuments, shafts and statues to the memory of tsars dead and gone. Petrograd affected Scorpio with a strong sense of melancholy. The city was beautiful, full of history, but he sensed, not always a happy place. In a strange way it reminded him of his home city, though it was half underwater and looked nothing at all like this one. He had been away so long that at times he gave up all hope of seeing his own world again, but when familiar places came back to him in memory, he reaffirmed his desire to return.

The hotel that the brothers had chosen was in a district much different from those they had passed earlier. The streets were filled, even at this hour, with unshaven loiterers, some of them wearing ragged army uniforms. Vasha and Misha had brought a bottle of vodka, and in their hotel room they spent the rest of the evening swapping the bottle back and forth in a peaceable kind of Russian roulette.

When the brothers were sprawled on the floor and snoring loudly sometime later, Scorpio realized that if he wished to, he could escape. Thinking of the dark street and the suspicious-looking men inhabiting it, he decided to cast his lot with the brothers, at least for the moment.

He covered them with extra blankets, and since they were not using the bed, he claimed it for his own. Surprisingly, in this cheap room, it was very soft and comfortable.

A few days later Scorpio had to try and control the anxiety that made him want to bolt, as he and the brothers waited at the servants' entrance of a handsome townhouse. Like most of the buildings of the city, it was of stone. Since the city had been built above a swamp, enormous foundations were needed, giving the buildings an even more imposing look.

The lanky black-clothed butler who opened the door to them looked startled to find three roughly dressed men, one of them with his face covered.

Vasha asked for Mme. Sverdlova.

"Does Madame know you?" he asked. He spoke Russian with an accent, and had such a haughty expression frozen on his face that Scorpio wondered if it caused him pain.

"No, but I know she's interested in spirits, and I think she might like to meet our friend here," said Vasha, indicating Scorpio.

"I really doubt if she would," said the butler, "and Madame is interested in spiritualism, not spirits."

"Spiritualism, spirits, what's the difference?" said Vasha. "Pull down the muffler," he hissed at Scorpio who slowly unwound it, exposing his face. "Our friend Scorpio here is a genuine *Lesovik*, from the Siberian taiga, and he's a talented healer, much renowned in the village of Tutalsk for his cures."

The butler stared for a moment. "He is ... somewhat remarkable," he said. "Perhaps Madame—wait right here."

After a time the butler returned and invited them in. "You must wait here, in the kitchen," he said, looking at the trail of mud and slush they were leaving on the clean tile floor.

A girl in a black and white maid's costume was taking her ease by a table and she looked at them with frank curiosity.

A few minutes later Mme. Sverdlova entered with a flutter. This was partly because she affected a style of dress that leaned heavily toward layers of diaphanous material and partly because she seemed to be in a constant state of activity. She was tall and thin, with a chignon of rustred hair. Scorpio could not have guessed how old she was, though there were definite lines around her dark, expressive eyes.

The brothers had been told about her in a tavern they had frequented. Some of their drinking companions had read stories about her in the newspapers. She was the wife of a minor government functionary and an heiress in her own right, but her chief claim to notoriety was as a theosophist and psychic medium.

"This is all very irregular, Hookes, I'm in the middle of having tea with my Society of Sensitives. Why are these low-class brutes messing up my clean kitchen? What was so important that it couldn't—" Then she spotted Scorpio.

"Who or what is this?" she asked.

"This is Scorpio," said Vasha, and repeated his *Lesovik* spiel, though Mme. Sverdlova didn't look convinced. She did look intrigued, however.

"What are you? Do you speak," she asked, leaning so close that her sickly sweet perfume washed over him. Her thickly powdered face seemed magnified, making him queasy.

"Yes, I do," he said.

Startled by the response, Mme. Sverdlova nearly fell backward. Then she composed herself, smoothed the front of her elaborate black satin afternoon dress. "Hookes, take Scorpio up to the spare room and see if you can't outfit him properly to take tea with us. These other two" —her face screwed up in a look of faint disgust—"pay them some money so that they'll go away." She turned to leave and then seemed to notice the maidservant for the first time.

"Yvonne, you lazy girl. Didn't I tell you to go and stand in the queues for bread and sugar? If you're late, they're sure to be sold out."

Galvanized into action, the maid nodded vigorously and left.

"It's bad enough that there's not enough food and I have to hire a maidservant just to spend time standing in a queue in the hope of buying some. All these silly ideas of freedom and equality are spoiling the help," complained Mme. Sverdlova to no one in particular. "What are things coming to?"

"I'm not sure I want to stay here alone," said Scorpio quietly to Vasha. Taking tea with Mme. Sverdlova and her friends sounded like one of those human social occasions that always unnerved him.

"Don't worry, we'll be back later on," said Vasha. "The nice man is going to give us thirty rubles to get rid of us."

"Twenty," said Hookes.

"Twenty-five."

"All right," agreed Hookes.

"Now make a good impression on Madame and her friends," said Vasha. "Or else."

Scorpio stood before the full-length mirror studying his reflection. The suit, cut for a normal human being, fit him oddly. The collar, which was made of some kind of plastic, dug into his neck.

"Madame suggested you might also wear this," said Hookes, handing him a large purple turban with an ostrich plume.

Scorpio had not imagined he could look worse until he donned the headgear.

"Very handsome," said Hookes. Scorpio couldn't imagine how the man kept from laughing out loud. Scorpio imagined he must have learned that in butler school at the same time he learned to look haughty.

When Scorpio was conducted to the salon, he tried to enter inconspicuously, or as inconspicuously as one could, tricked out in a purple turban. Those in the room stopped talking as he entered, and then there was a flurry of subdued conversation.

Mme. Sverdlova tapped her teacup with her spoon. "Everyone, allow me to introduce my latest protégé: Scorpio, a famous psychic and healer, who has just arrived here from Siberia."

There was another short silence and then the guests began to applaud.

"See, you're already a great success," whispered Mme. Sverdlova.

"I haven't done anything yet," said Scorpio.

"Don't worry about that. Just mingle with my guests. You'll be a sensation." She added with a smirk, "And so will I."

Scorpio wasn't certain what "mingling" with the guests entailed, so he only stood where he was. Hookes, bearing a tray, pressed a teacup into his hand. It turned out that he didn't have to do anything; he was soon surrounded by several fine ladies vying to be first to engage him in conversation.

He noticed that though the silver tea service was elegant, all the ladies carried their own small gold and silver and jeweled boxes for sugar, as if each had brought her own.

"We theosophists believe in reincarnation: that the soul is reborn in different eras of time," said a plump lady in a violet velvet gown who peered at him through a lorgnette. "Do you think it's possible you have lived before, in other times, Scorpio."

"Oh, I know I have," he said naively. "The Elizabethan Age, for one. I met her."

"Her? Oh, you mean that in an earlier life you met the Queen. How fascinating. What was she like?"

"Very nice, actually. She wore a red wig. And before that, there was fourteenth-century Avignon. That was a pretty interesting time. Pope Clement tried to have me killed."

"Do you hear that, Scorpio remembers the events of his past lives," said another lady shrilly.

"Well, it was not all that long ago—" he began, but the ladies were chattering at each other in excitement.

After that it didn't matter much what he said. They were ready to be impressed.

"What is the latest news about Rasputin?" asked a guest later, when the talk had turned to other topics.

"I have heard that he influenced the Tsar to name Varnava as Archbishop of Tobolsk," said Mme. Sverdlova. "Everyone knows that Varnava was only an illiterate gardener's son before he became a monk."

"His greatest crime was in recommending Protopopov as Minister of the Interior. Everyone knows the man is grossly incompetent."

"My dears," said Sverdlova, "it's a great scandal. Imagine it, Rasputin, a mere peasant, allowed the run of the palace and influencing the Tsar in such a way! Who has ever heard of such a thing?"

Scorpio had heard of Rasputin from Igor so he ventured an opinion. "I've heard he's a great healer. And that he has healed the Tsar's ailing son. Perhaps he has received his high position because of their gratitude."

"He has a reputation as a psychic and a healer, at any rate," said one of the guests. "And perhaps he *is* talented in that way. I have only seen him at a distance but there was something about his eyes. But if his motives were good in healing the boy, they are certainly unsavory in every other way."

"The Tsarina's reputation hasn't been improved by all this talk of Rasputin."

"That German woman, you mean. I don't see how she can be a patriot to Russia when her father was a German. With the Tsar at the front, she has free rein in the palace. Everyone knows she tries to rule the country in his stead. Probably she'd like to cause as much trouble as possible, so that we can be easily conquered."

"I hear that there are many German spies among us," said Mme. Sverdlova. "For example, it is said that Professor Mirskaya, who teaches physics at the University, was an assistant to Albert Einstein."

"I'm sorry, but I don't know who that is," said Scorpio.

"He is a German scientist reputed to be a genius at mathematics and physics. He's formulating a theory of space and time."

"Of space and time?" asked Scorpio, truly interested in this conversation for the first time.

"Of course it's probably just a cover for another horrible weapon the Kaiser is planning to use against our Russian boys."

"But this Professor Mirskaya really understands something of the nature of space and time?" asked Scorpio.

"I've heard that Daria Nicolaevna Mirskaya is the most brilliant young scientist in Russia. It's a pity she has come under suspicion by having worked with a German."

• • •

After the guests had left, Mme. Sverdlova and Scorpio sat amid the wrack of the tea table as several servants began to clear things away. "This was a *most* successful afternoon," said Mme. Sverdlova. "And I owe a great deal of it to you."

"I did very little, actually."

"Your appearance gives you a certain advantage, but it was a brilliant stroke to let it slip that you remembered your past lives. You have great potential, Scorpio, but let us remember that it is contact with the right people that will allow you to realize that potential. Rasputin would still be behind a plow in Siberia if Anna Virubova had not introduced him at court. I have a friend or two at court myself. And in theosophist circles I am highly regarded. I was even in correspondence with Aleister Crowley, the famous British mage, for a time. Perhaps you would like to see the letters. They are fascinating."

"Oh, no, that's not necessary."

"The Tsarevitch is still quite ill. Perhaps you could help him."

"I'm afraid I can do little as a healer just now," said Scorpio, "though I'm always glad to do what I can to help the sick."

"You're too modest, I'm sure."

"But it's getting late. I must get out of these clothes. The Mishkin brothers will be returning soon."

"I'm afraid I have instigated a slight deception," said Mme. Sverdlova with an impish grin. "Your companions returned for you over an hour ago, but I instructed Hookes to tell them you had decided you would be residing here at my invitation." Her constantly gesturing hands spread out to indicate the lavish appointments of the room. "I do invite you to stay here. I don't really know what your relationship was to those two loafers, but I dare say they would have had you appearing as a sideshow act for two kopeks a peep."

"I don't owe them any loyalty," said Scorpio. "After all, one thinking being cannot own another."

"That's quite true." Mme. Sverdlova turned to the girl who was clearing the table. "Nadia, how many times have I told you to be careful of the china. I can hear the cups clashing together like cymbals. Anything broken comes out of your wages!"

Returning her attention to Scorpio, she said, "I think you've made a wise decision."

"I have but one condition."

"Yes?"

"I refuse to wear this!" he said, holding out the garish turban.

"I thought it was quite dramatic, but as you wish. And if you are to be seen in my circles, I must do something about those dreadfully fitting clothes. I will have my husband's tailor take your measurements to provide something more suitable."

Later, as he relaxed in a hot, scented bath, Scorpio was cheered by the news of the woman scientist Daria Nicolaevna Mirskaya. It sounded very promising, a scientist working on a theory of space and time. This was no wild-eyed magician or shaman, but someone who could very well help him understand the workings of the orb.

In a more humorous mood he imagined the angry scene that must have occurred at the servants' entrance when Hookes relayed the message to the brothers Mishkin.

Now they would have to give up their dreams of glory and look for honest work. Somehow he didn't think they were up to the task.

But he had his own problems. After a while Mme. Sverdlova wasn't going to be satisfied with the stir his mere appearance caused among her friends. Someone was sure to ask for proof he was a healer, and he could do little without the orb.

He spent much of the evening concentrating deeply. Though he felt no contact, he hoped Leah was all right.

Chapter Five

The Finland Station was nothing like the small station where Leah had boarded the train. It was immense, its vaulted ceilings making it look almost like a cathedral, only grimier. Inside, people of all types jostled together, as if in a great hurry.

Leah had never seen this sort of intensity before, not even on the faces of farmers bringing their produce into the city on market day. It was as if the noise and velocity of the train had somehow affected the people's minds. That was what you got, she decided, for moving at speeds far beyond what the human body could comfortably stand.

The crowds were funneling toward the gate where two men in uniform stood checking passports and papers. Leah felt her stomach knot up with anxiety.

They paused by a bench. There, Botchkareva took a handful of coins from Leah's hoard and dropped them into the envelope her own papers had been in. Leah wondered what would happen if Botchkareva were wrong about the bribe. Maybe they would both be arrested.

However, the woman seemed confident, showing her own papers to the officials and then conferring quietly with them. When she handed the agent the envelope, he peered inside and quickly closed it again, nodding his head for Leah to pass.

"We made it," she said thankfully as they paused outside the station. "But how will I make my way through the city without papers? I don't have enough money to bribe everyone."

"I do know of a place," said Botchkareva, "where passports and identities can be acquired for a price." She whispered the address and Leah memorized it.

They were standing near the street and Leah heard a strange noise like the squawk of a mechanical fowl, and she was hit by a wave of slush. When she looked behind her, she was too startled by what she saw to be angry. It was a vehicle shaped roughly like a carriage, but riding much lower to the ground, its fat wheels carrying it along. Like the train, it had no horses hitched to it. It made an awful racket and shot out a plume of smoke as it sped off down the street.

"What are you staring at?" asked Botchkareva. "One would think you'd never seen a motor car."

"It just looks so strange, that's all," said Leah.

"You'll get used to the sight if you're here long. That reminds me of the tale they tell about the moujik who saw a phonograph for the first time. He simply wanted to go lie down under a bush and die. I hope you don't have similar feelings. Well, I must be on my way."

"Yes, and I should do something about my lack of a passport as soon as I can," said Leah, turning to go.

"Don't take one of these droshkies," advised Botchkareva, gesturing toward the horse-drawn cabs lined up along the street. "The *Izvoschiki* ask an extra high price from those leaving the station; newcomers don't know any better than to pay it. Walk two blocks that way and you can catch a streetcar. Much cheaper."

"Thanks for your help," said Leah. "I hope all goes well for you when you return to the front."

"N'chevo," said the woman soldier with a shrug. Leah would hear the phrase often; it indicated a patient acceptance of one's fate. Along with the shrug and stolid expression, it seemed somehow to sum up the character of the Russian people.

A Petrograd street was not the place for long goodbyes, Leah realized. A frigid, snow-laden wind swept along between massive and ornate buildings, making her pull her sheepskin coat closer about her. She began to walk quickly in the direction Botchkareva had indicated.

She didn't know what a streetcar was, but when she saw the monster of clattering metal as it meandered along, following the cable strung overhead, it no longer looked so frightening or surprising. It seemed a distant cousin of the train, but it didn't move so quickly.

It slewed to a stop and people raced toward the open doors. Leah was not so intimidated by the crowd this time, and she quickly made her way inside. All the seats were taken, many of them with men in disheveled uniforms. *Deserters?* she wondered. *Or soldiers on leave?* None of them offered her a seat, so she was forced to cling to a strap hanging from the ceiling as many others on board had to do.

The streetcar moved snail-like with a groaning noise over the snow-packed street. She saw another motor car go past, passing horse-drawn vehicles with the same sort of squawking noise that had frightened her earlier. The address she had been given was an apartment house near the Vyborg district, which seemed to be a collection of grimy barracklike buildings with smokestacks trailing gritty plumes into a colorless sky. When she asked a fellow passenger about them, he said, "Factories," and lapsed into silence, as if that explained everything.

Half-frozen and hanging on her strap like a side of beef hung in a smokehouse, she thought briefly of Scorpio, and wondered how he was faring in the city. The situation didn't allow her to concentrate deeply. Once she had purchased an identity and found a place to stay, she could try and pinpoint where Scorpio had been taken.

The apartment house was of the same smoke-begrimed brick as all the structures in the area. When she rapped at the door, an adolescent boy with furtive eyes in a sooty, wizened face opened it. The boy looked as though he belonged in this neighborhood, as if proximity to these factories had leached out all his youthful vigor, making him old before his time. She would learn that each apartment house had its own *dvornik*, or doorkeeper, who was also responsible for keeping the pavement before the building free of snow and for bringing in firewood for the stoves. This one looked at her stupidly as she repeated the name she had been given, until she produced a coin and placed it in his hand.

"Oh, you want to see Radek," he said, a gleam of understanding appearing in his deep-set eyes.

She was taken to an office the size of a closet and left there. For all the speed of the train, she was beginning to realize that some things moved quite slowly. She supposed this Radek had to be some sort of criminal; maybe he was even dangerous.

After she had had sufficient time to worry, a slight, young man with tousled black hair entered. He wore small round spectacles and a dusty black workman's blouse with the sleeves rolled up. She noticed that black stains were deeply ingrained on his hands. She thought at first it was grease, and then realized it was ink.

"I'm David Radek," he said. The expression on his fine-boned face was sober and intense.

"I need an identity," said Leah.

Then Radek smiled, looking at her speculatively over his glasses. "Why, have you lost your own?"

"No, I'm who I always was, it's just things around me that have changed," she said.

"Touché," he said, laughing, as if she had been joking. "One might say that honestly of us all, I suppose. Who do you want to be?"

"Well, I don't know. My name is Leah de Bernay."

He wrote it on a piece of paper and said, "Nationality, French. Nothing wrong with that; we have quite a few foreigners living among us. Some of them are French. Religion?"

Leah hesitated, then said, "I'm a Jew." She hadn't intended to because in her travels she had come to realize that not everyone was pleased to hear this. But she didn't like hiding it, either; that felt like a betrayal.

"Since you can have anything you want on here, you might want to reconsider," said Radek in such a bitter tone that she stared at him. "Some things are forbidden to Jews in our society."

"Then they are forbidden to me, too."

"As you wish," he said, scribbling it on his paper. He studied her a moment. "You're young, and no peasant, despite the clothes you wear. Suppose I give you the passport of a university student."

"That sounds fine."

"It's plausible to say you're attending classes at the University of Petrograd."

"Can you make my studies medicine?" she asked. "I suppose that's silly because this is only a make-believe identity, but—"

"Anything you like. I went to the University myself for a while, studying law. Then, because of the *numerus clausus*, the quota of Jews allowed at the University, I was dropped. It probably doesn't matter; I suppose I wasn't such a good student anyway. At any rate, I've found a better profession. Lawyers can only work within the law."

"You're a Jew? But I thought you said your name was Radek?"

"That is a name I chose for myself. It is done often in my profession. Ulianov changes his name to Lenin, Bron-stein becomes Trotsky."

Leah found all the name-changing odd, but she supposed when one worked in the profession of false passports and papers, mendacity became second nature.

When he had finished writing, Radek pushed the paper across the desk to her as if to invite her to see if everything was correct. She studied it silently.

"You can read?"

She nodded.

"That's very lucky. I was just thinking—well, there is a job for someone who can read. It pays little, but—"

"I need a job," said Leah. Her money had been dwindling and her search for Scorpio might take weeks or longer. "Is it at a school?"

"Sort of. It's in the basement of a building a few doors down. The factory workers come there late at night to learn to read."

Leah gave him a puzzled look.

"I suppose I must tell you that teaching the workers to read isn't a popular activity where the police are concerned. There could be an element of danger to it."

"I do need a job," she said, "and a place to stay, as well."

"That's not a problem. There's an empty flat in this building. I'll have the *dvornik* show it to you."

"Well, I think I've got it working again," said someone behind Leah. She turned and saw a stocky red-haired man with a broad good-natured peasant face.

I'm glad to hear it." Radek seemed a little reluctant, but he introduced the intruder as Stefan Pugatchev. When Stefan reached out and shook hands, Leah's hand almost disappeared in his huge paw. She realized that the stains on his shirtfront and hands really *were* grease. She had some of it on her fingers when he let go.

As Leah went up the narrow stairs behind the *dvornik*, she felt suspicious. She no longer thought Radek was a criminal, at least not one of the dangerous sort, but things had worked out a little too handily.

In the meantime, she did need a job and a place to stay. Ivan, the *dvornik*, led the way down a hall and through a door into what looked like a cage of brass. A squat woman in a black dress, her hair tied up in a babushka, sat on a stool in one corner holding two metal levers. A semicircle of sunflower seed husks lay about her feet.

"Four," said Ivan, and to Leah's horror the cage door shut with a bang, the woman did something to the levers, and the room began to move upward slowly, with a wheezing noise. Leah felt panic and wanted to scream, but since the others were taking this all calmly, she restrained herself. After a few moments the cage had reached the proper floor and the door opened again.

Glad to have escaped from this trap, but wondering how she would get down from here, Leah followed Ivan to another, more solid and reassuring door. He used his key to open it and a scent of mustiness greeted them. Large brown waterstains and clinging patches of green mildew climbed all the plaster walls and the board floor was warped. The few pieces of furniture looked faded and dispirited after years of hard use.

"Lights here," said the *dvornik*, and Leah was startled as he touched a button on the wall and light washed over everything. It emanated from a glass ball hanging on a cord from the ceiling. She tried to stare into the heart of the light. It was not flame, but something else. It burned steadily, coldly, making her eyes water.

"Electricity is only on from six to ten o'clock," Ivan was saying. "Power is scarce, and in any case we don't want to be a target for any zeppelins passing overhead. Keep these blinds pulled."

Zeppelins passing overhead, Leah echoed in her mind, but she decided she didn't want to know right now. After all she'd seen so far, nothing could be a surprise.

He moved into a very small room, and she heard the gush of water as he moved one lever and then another. "Hot. Cold," he said. "Well, maybe cold, cold is more like it. But at least everything works." He pulled a chain hanging at one side of the room and Leah almost jumped as a swoosh of water came from a porcelain bowl below it.

After Ivan had left, Leah amused herself for some time by turning the magic light on and off and causing water to gush from the faucets and commode. What king or pope in Avignon had such luxury? But after her first day here she was exhausted and almost sated on wonders. Maybe that peasant had a point about wanting to go off and die under a bush. It felt good to just have a warm place to sit and rest.

She took the orb out of her valise and unwrapped the thick layer of furs she had put around it. The precautions she had taken must have protected it because it gleamed a pure radiant gold. "You seem to be in good health; not that it does me any particular good," she said, addressing it, as she had seen Scorpio do when he didn't think she was watching. She knew that the thing wouldn't answer her, but it was rather like a companion, in a way.

Using it as a point of focus, she began to try and concentrate on Scorpio. She was too tired and kept nodding off over the orb without ever making contact.

Chapter Six

Leah settled in. Teaching the workers from nearby factories wasn't the hardest work she'd ever had to do, but sometimes it felt strange hearing great hulking bearded men haltingly read from a child's primer. Some of her pupils were women or children. Children evidently worked in the factories, too, and their grimy clothes and pinched, weary expressions made Leah long to take them home to clean them up and give them a hot meal. Every time period she had so far visited had these signs of poverty, as if want were a consistent part of human life no matter what the place or time.

The school at which she taught was held in the dank basement of an empty building. Others did this work, too. She began to recognize the other teachers as tenants in her apartment building. Occasionally Radek would take a turn at the school, but most of the time she saw him only sporadically, always intent on some secret mission.

One day, late in the afternoon, she was just gathering up her books when she saw someone standing in the doorway watching her. Remembering what she had been told about the danger of this work, she felt a touch of fear until she recognized Pugatchev and remembered meeting him earlier in Radek's office.

"Hello, Stefan," she said. "Did you come to give me a message from Radek?"

"I'm not his messenger," he said, smiling, "although I do have an important job to do. I wondered if you'd care to go with me. I'm off to hang these posters on every wall and kiosk in the city." She saw that he carried a stack of freshly printed posters under his arm and in his other hand, a bucket of glue and a brush.

"That sounds ambitious," she said.

"Or as many as I can reach in an hour or so," he amended.

Feeling logy from hours spent poring over letters and numbers, the idea of fresh air and seeing more of the city appealed to Leah. Stefan seemed congenial enough.

"All right, I'll go," she said.

As they went out, Leah saw that the clouds had cleared away, leaving the sky a clear, intense blue. Cold sunlight accentuated the layers of soot on everything. As they walked along, she noticed that the shops had pictographs for signs. *It looks as if my work as a teacher isn't going to make much of a dent in illiteracy,* she thought. It was unbelievable to her that these people could rush around in magical conveyances and speak across vast distances, and yet many of them could hardly write their own names. They passed several stores that were boarded up. Those that were still open had people standing in long lines before their doors, as if waiting to make a purchase.

Pugatchev only shrugged when she indicated one of these queues. "Everything is in short supply these days because of the corruption of government. That's why we must do something."

He chose a promising-looking blank wall and slapped some glue on it. Leah helped him mash the poster flat against the bricks of the wall and in doing so read a passage from it,

Workers, throw off the yoke of the autocracy. Let your voices be heard in demanding a new and more progressive society ...

• • •

There was a lot more, but all the same. She didn't know all that much about the situation here, but the words of the poster were clearly seditious. They found a few more good spots and pasted up some more of the posters, but Leah was beginning to worry about the message on them. She was about to ask Pugatchev whether what they were doing was legal when she heard a shout.

"Stop! Stand where you are in the name of the law!"

As she turned to look, she saw two men approaching. They were dressed in impressive uniforms with shiny buttons and gold braid. Her question became unnecessary as she saw Pugatchev drop the posters and glue.

"The Blacklegs are coming. Run!" he shouted at her, and took to his heels.

Leah began to run, but she couldn't match her companion's pace. After half a block, she found herself falling far behind him. The policemen hadn't given up. She could hear them pounding along, gaining on her. Luckily, Pugatchev had run back in the direction they had come. Leah began to recognize details she had taken note of as they had passed this way. In Elizabethan England she had been trained by a master thief to keep a sharp eye out for hiding places.

Knowledge of an area gave the thief an advantage when it came time to flee the authorities. She didn't really know this area well, since there had been little time to explore it, but she remembered a stone archway they had come through and raced toward it now, her breath rattling in her throat. The arch had a panel of bas-relief ornamentation. She had noticed earlier that there was a space between this and the top of the archway itself. The stones had shifted over the years, leaving the surface rough, with many protuberances. She thought she could do it. There would be only one chance.

As she reached the archway, instead of proceeding through it, she climbed monkeylike up the rock protrusions. She huddled in the small space at the top, perching on the struts that supported the bas-relief. She heard the heavy footsteps of the policemen, the rasp of their breathing, and hoped intently that they were looking straight ahead. She wouldn't be quite out of sight here for someone looking up. Their running footsteps continued on through the arch and on up the street. *It's a good thing you can run fast, Pugatchev,* she thought. *Because now they're on your trail, not mine.*

Radek hardly noticed that Pugatchev had entered, because of the steady noise of the printing press. It was an idiosyncratic press, built of the pieces and parts of other old machines. Though it made an awful racket, there was something comforting to him in its noise and the smell of fresh ink as leaflets came through the rollers in an inexhaustible stream—to him it was a never-ending miracle to see the crisp black letters appearing on white paper, bringing the fresh air of ideas to the ignorant. He turned to see Pugatchev, disheveled, red-faced and panting.

"Blacklegs—caught us—with the posters. I got away—but I don't know about her—"

"Her? Who went with you? I thought you usually went on these errands alone."

"The new one—you know her—long black hair—big eyes—small waist," he measured with his hands.

"Leah. You mean Leah. You idiot! She knows nothing of our operation. She was surely caught and who knows what will happen to her!"

"I didn't say she was caught," said Pugatchev. "I looked back and the two policemen were chasing me. It was as if she disappeared."

"How do you know there weren't other police there?"

"Well, I don't, but—"

"How could you expose her to danger like that?"

"Look, you're just mad because you're interested in her yourself. I know that you agreed to give her false papers right off, without the usual screening."

It was true that no one seeking false identification was usually given what they wanted on the first visit. It was easy enough to tell them they had made a mistake and then have a confederate follow them for a while to see what their real motives were. There were all sorts of informers and spies about these days, glad to betray the revolutionary cause for a few rubles.

But for some reason he hadn't wanted to turn Leah away. She was different from anyone he had ever met. He got the feeling that she was on her own and vulnerable in an unfamiliar place. He had wanted to help her. Or maybe he had just liked her big eyes and little waist, like Pugatchev did, and became careless. What did it matter? It was the place of a revolutionary to develop instincts, to take risks.

There was the sound of shouting outside the door and when he opened it, he saw Leah and Ivan, the *dvornik*, arguing loudly.

"I told her that no one was allowed down here," said the *dvornik*, "but she wouldn't listen."

"That's all right. Let her come in."

Leah sidestepped the *dvornik* and entered, rage implicit in her every move. "You tricked me," she said, either to him or to Pugatchev, he wasn't sure. Maybe to both of them. The printing press, still clacking away in the middle of the room, drew her attention momentarily, as if it made her so curious, she couldn't sustain her anger, then with an effort, she gathered her forces and attacked again. "Those posters were fomenting sedition. Overthrow of the government!"

"What did you think you were doing day after day when you taught workers and the poor to read?" asked Pugatchev. "Our government would much prefer that they stay ignorant and easy to control."

"You're saying they couldn't read your seditious posters unless I taught them to read first. But I didn't know what was going on out there until the police came. You saved yourself and left me to be caught. Not exactly a gallant act."

"But you weren't caught, were you, *tovarish?"*

The word he had used, "comrade," cut through Leah's anger for the moment. The men she had known before had coddled and deferred to women but only because they thought them a weak, inferior sort of creature. While she wasn't quite sure that Pugatchev really had equality on his mind when he ran off and left her to the police, the idea of being called a "comrade," an equal partner in any endeavor, intrigued her.

As she thought this over, Leah's attention was wavering back toward the printing press, her anger beginning to dissipate. "So, this is what you do here. And do the other people in the building know this is going on. That nice elderly couple, Mr. and Mrs. Zahadin—"

"Have been linchpins of the revolution for thirty years."

"What about the Englishman who is here to set up a bicycle factory?"

"His 'business' is to keep an eye on the activities of the police and report it to us."

"All of them working for the revolution? Even Ivan the *dvornik?"*

"He is our courier."

"Old Katya?"

Radek smiled. "Katya runs the elevator. And chews sunflower seeds."

Leah sighed, walking closer to inspect the press.

"I'm running a new set of leaflets," said Radek. He picked up one and handed it to her. She seemed entranced by the moving parts of the machine and the way copy after perfect copy was piled up.

"I first learned of this machine in England," she said, "but I never thought I'd get to see one. Just imagine it. All these copies dispersed, people everywhere reading the same message. It's a miracle."

"I think so, too," said Radek.

"It's nothing, just something I put together from a collection of scrap parts," said Pugatchev, as if they had expressed admiration for him, personally, "like this other thing I've been working on." He crossed the room and pulled a cover off a jumble of mechanical parts in the center of which was a carriagelike shape. Leah realized it resembled the motor cars she'd seen earlier. She wondered if Pugatchev could really make this sort of magic. But if he was really responsible for the clattering printing press that continued to spew out leaflets, she had no choice other than to believe him.

"It doesn't seem as if a motor car would be much use in a basement," said Leah.

Pugatchev laughed and pointed to a stone ramp leading up to a set of wooden doors. "Those doors are on street level at the rear of the building. When I'm finished I can drive it right out of here. We'll have our own motor car, like the government higher-ups. We can take our leaflets and posters all over the city."

Once Leah had seen the printing press and what it could do, she seemed fascinated with it and spent as much time as possible helping Radek produce his revolutionary literature. Because of this, Radek felt she was a disciple in the making and he took every opportunity to enhance her education.

Radek pointed to the golden spire of the Admiralty topped by a weathervane in the shape of a ship. The spire rose into the sky at the point where three main avenues converged: the Nevsky Prospect, Dzerjinski Street and the Mairov Prospect. "Wherever you go in Petrograd, you can get your bearings from it," said Radek. "It's a symbol, too. It was here that Peter the Great affirmed his decision to open the seas to Russia."

They stood in the western exit from the Admiralty. On a huge block of carven stone Leah saw a statue of a rider on a prancing horse, a serpent being trampled beneath the horse's hooves, at the same time obligingly creating a support for the horse's tail. "It is called Decembrists' Square because it was here in December 1825 that the first battle of our revolution took place. A secret society had carefully laid their plans to subvert the army to their cause, and the Moskovy regiment was the first to declare rebellion."

As he spoke, Leah imagined those soldiers marching out into the square on a bright, cold day, drums rolling and regimental colors flying. The people in the streets would be cheering them on, some of them joining the procession with makeshift weapons, everyone hoping that this act would lead to freedom and a better life for all.

"But the plans of the secret society had gone awry. Six thousand troops were needed to overcome the loyalists and barely three thousand stood in the square, hoping vainly that others would join them. The Tsar delayed, hoping the men would come to their senses, but he knew he couldn't allow them to remain there until night, for by that time other troops might join them. After attempting to negotiate, he was forced to order the artillery into position."

"They wouldn't shoot their own men," said Leah.

"The gun crew didn't want to. At first they fired into the air, hitting the upper floor of the Senate. Then they were ordered to fire at the rebels."

Leah imagined the confusion, the roar of the guns and the rattle of musket fire. Horses screaming and falling on the icy cobblestones.

"Few prisoners were taken and most of the wounded were shot where they lay, but the worst was what came after. All night a crew of the Tsar's men worked feverishly to cleanse the Senate Square of every sign of the battle. When the sun came up, there were no bodies, no bloodstains, no marks of canister and grapeshot, no bullet holes. A person passing by would see nothing to suggest that any uprising had occurred."

"They buried the bodies so quickly?"

"That problem was solved by throwing all the bodies into the river; some of the wounded were thrown in as well. Of course, in the spring when the ice melted, bodies were seen floating on the Neva."

Leah shivered, remembering her run-in with the Blacklegs, the police of the Tsar. At the time it had seemed something of an adventure; but now, hearing how casually ruthless the tsars could be, she had a new appreciation for her narrow escape.

"But don't look so grim, I have a present for you," said Radek, bringing out a carefully wrapped parcel.

Leah opened it up and saw a bright red kerchief. "It's beautiful," she said, and then laughed. Because of a trick of language, she had also said, "It's red."

"Red is the color of revolution," said Radek, stopping her as she was about to tie it on her head. "So, for now, you should put it away and admire it, until the day you can wear it everywhere. That day won't be long in coming, I promise!"

• • •

That evening Leah tied the scarf on her head and peered into the tarnished glass of the mirror in her bedroom. Only a small oil lamp illuminated the room, and her face was an indistinct oval amid gathering shadows. She remembered watching Radek as he retold the story of that early revolution. It was as if he relived it as he spoke. He wasn't gallant or handsome. He didn't dress in the latest fashion, like the men she had admired in the past. Yet there was something about him ...

She smiled secretively at her reflection.

But why are you standing here daydreaming like a lovesick schoolgirl when Scorpio is still a captive? The question crowded into her mind, dispelling her romantic fancies. It was no doubt only her conscience nagging at her. Yet she looked around the room as if someone else were there, influencing her thoughts. She opened a dresser drawer and a shaft of light emerged into the room's dimness. *All right, I came here to rescue Scorpio, and that's what I'm going to do.* She sat crosslegged on the bed, the orb cradled in her hands. After what must have been hours, her eyes blurred and swam with golden afterimages, and she felt the beginning of a pounding headache. That was all.

On another occasion Leah and Radek stood across the Neva from the gleaming golden spire that marked the Fortress of St. Peter and St. Paul. "You remember," said Radek, "that I once told you that there were many who plotted the overthrow of the government since the uprising in

Decembrists' Square, but of all of them, Nechayev was my hero. He was the greatest revolutionary of them all.

"The Tsar imprisoned him there, in the Fortress, thinking he would cause no further trouble. For over twenty years he was a captive, but for most of that time, he cleverly subverted the guards to his purposes and had messages smuggled out to his followers. When his plots were finally uncovered and he was suffering from diseases caused by poor food and confinement, he asked the Tsar to allow him one request: a Bible and a priest to hear his confession. The Tsar refused, saying that he would find some way to use the pages of the Bible to write messages, and the priest to smuggle them out." Radek laughed. "And he probably would have, too."

"Did he escape?"

"No, there was simply no more word from him. Rumors flew as to his fate, but finally word leaked out that he had died in his cell, from the diseases."

Leah leaned closer to Radek as a chill wind blew across the ice. She felt her eyes burning with tears, partly for the man she could never know, who had suffered and died alone for his ideals, but partly because this seemed something that Radek wanted to share with her. She had never felt closer to him, and she was happy when he put an arm around her shoulders. She closed her eyes, waiting to feel his lips on hers.

But instead she felt something pressed into her hand. She looked down and saw that it was a piece of paper. The sheet was yellowed with age and so creased that it was practically falling apart.

"That is the revolutionary catechism written by Nechayev himself," said Radek. "I've tried to live by it, and by the memory of Nechayev and all the others who gave their lives."

Later, in her flat, she read the catechism over in its entirety. It was a sort of guidebook for anyone who wanted to live the life of a revolutionary. She supposed it made a great deal of sense for one who had decided to devote his life to revolution, but for herself she found it rather harsh. One passage haunted her thoughts: "All the soft and tender affections arising from kinship, friendship and love ... must be obliterated."

Only someone inhuman could really live by that, she thought, refolding the paper carefully and putting it away. *Only someone inhuman* ... This turned her thoughts to Scorpio again. She had tried several times to contact him, yet there was no response. She didn't like the thought that crept into her mind but had to admit it was a possibility. If something had happened to Scorpio, if he were dead, that might explain why all her efforts to make contact had failed.

Quickly she got the orb. As if doing penance for even considering the idea of Scorpio's death, she spent the next two hours concentrating. Two wasted hours.

One day Radek had finished showing Leah another point of historical interest, when she turned to him and said, "There's one place in the city where we've never gone," she said. "And that's to your home in the Jewish sector. Do you never go back there?"

"I go, sometimes," he said, though it had been almost a year since he'd last visited his parents. "I'm afraid I don't fit in very well there anymore. I'm helping to create a new world, but nothing ever changes there."

"I hoped you'd say that," said Leah. "Can we go sometime?"

Radek grudgingly told her yes, hoping she would forget about it. Since she didn't forget and kept reminding him, one morning he arranged for the visit. My parents are going to be confused, he thought. After all our arguments about giving up my faith to work for the revolution, the last thing they'd expect is for me to bring home a nice Jewish girl.

The streetcar slowly groaned along through the Jewish sector. Leah was appalled to see that poverty was even worse here than in the factory district where she lived. A few shops they passed still flourished, but most were only burnt-out skeletons with boards nailed over the windows and doors.

"My father had a shop in this neighborhood a few years ago," said Radek. "It was a thriving business. Then there was a raid by the Black Hundreds and his shop was destroyed. He was lucky to escape with his life, I suppose. Of course earlier pogroms were much worse; now the violence is only sporadic. Still, if it affects you personally—"

"What are the Black Hundreds?"

"An anti-Semitic group."

"But doesn't the government do something about them?"

"The Tsar supports them. He is himself a member of the League of Russian People, another hate group. He allows the publication of their anti-Semitic literature. It is not a bad strategy. If the Russian people can be convinced the Jews are to blame for their troubles, that takes the blame for hard times off the Tsar's inept government, where it really belongs."

"As you told me, nothing ever changes here," said Leah, thinking of how her own people in Avignon had been blamed for the Plague.

"Since we live differently within a country, and keep to our own laws and religion, this tends to make governments very nervous. It's easy to stir up the people against us because of what they think are barbaric religious customs. If a corpse is found, no matter what the cause of death, the rumors begin. They will tell that the body was found drained of all its blood for some arcane Jewish ritual."

"Isn't there some way to fight back?"

"Yes, strangely enough, after ages of pacifism we began to organize and to fight in our own defense. We were more than a match for a few drunken raiders. The problem came when the Tsar's police stood by until the fight was over. Then they killed and arrested Jews for using violence in defending themselves. You see, whether we obeyed the Tsar's law or broke it, we couldn't win."

Radek lapsed into silence, and Leah said no more, afraid to further disturb old memories. They entered a small, dimly lit house, suffused with Sabbath calm. The furnishings were different from those in the house of her childhood, but Leah felt immediately at home as she saw candles softly burning and goblets of wine set out on a table covered in antique lace. Radek was greeted somewhat formally by a slim, stooped gray-haired man and a small, neat woman with a corona of braided hair. They were polite to each other, but it was the politeness of strangers, Leah thought. Their conversation seemed guarded, as if they could not talk of certain things. Leah tried not to notice the strain between them, and concentrated on enjoying the visit. In her travels through time, there was something comforting about coming back to a place where traditions had not changed, even though the world around seemed warped out of shape and moving at a frightening pace.

"Well, we must be leaving," said Radek after a few hours had passed.

"So soon?" asked Leah, disappointment obvious on her face. Reluctantly she rose to go.

"But you will come back and visit us again," said Radek's father, seeing them to the door.

"Of course I will," said Leah. "If I can."

"I suppose I should go back and see my parents more," Radek said on their way home. "For some reason today wasn't quite as awkward as my visits usually are. Of course with you there, my father couldn't launch into one of his tirades about how I've given up my heritage.

"Not that he isn't right, I suppose, but he doesn't understand that Russia must be made a good place to live for all classes of society. Yes, Jews have suffered as much or more than most, but others are suffering, too."

Leah realized why she had been so reluctant to leave Radek's parents' home. In that quiet, well-kept parlor, it was possible to think of herself and Radek living together as man and wife, growing old together. It was an ordinary fantasy; millions of people lived that way.

But as she looked at Radek, it was hard to visualize him living the life of an ordinary man. He was intense, moody, with things on his mind that he wasn't able to express. Sometimes he made her angry, but he made her think. Before, she had simply accepted poverty and ignorance. Radek had forced her to see that, with struggle, people's lives might improve. But she was sometimes confused as to whether it was humanity or just Radek she loved.

Chapter Seven

Vasha rubbed his sore back and leaned on his shovel. Misha continued to scrape away at the frozen slush on the pavement before the glittering display in the window of the jewelry shop. Along the Nevsky Prospect, Petrograd's main thoroughfare of commerce, there were still shopkeepers with wares to sell to the rich and enough money to hire laborers to clean the snow from the pavement. This was only one in a series of menial jobs he and Misha had held.

"Brother, we can always go back to Tutalsk," said Misha, seeing Vasha's weary expression.

"What, go back in disgrace, knowing that renegade of a *Lesovik* tricked us!"

"It may have been Mme. Sverdlova, not Scorpio, who ordered the butler to send us packing," said Misha. "We carried off the gray man in the first place. Perhaps Mme. Sverdlova only did the same thing."

"Remember the night before last when we saw the two of them drive up before the Mariinsky Theatre where Karsavina is appearing in a new ballet? You saw that Scorpio was dressed like a dandy in a fine silk suit, handsome gold watch and chain, and spats. Did he look like a captive to you?"

"No, but—"

"Later, I saw a picture of Sverdlova in the newspaper. Someone read me the piece. It said they were holding seances and readings at her townhouse where the cream of Petrograd society gathers. He's taking advantage of the situation to make his fortune, just as we planned to do. He's probably laughing at us this minute while we break our backs on this job."

"There is little we can do about it," said Misha with a shrug, "as long as he is under Mme. Sverdlova's protection."

"We will bide our time. Perhaps there will be an opportunity. What—" A furtive figure passed him, hurrying into the jewelry shop. It had been muffled to the eyes in a long coat of badly cured sheepskins, with the collar pulled up and a fur hat pulled low. He had caught only a glimpse of the face, and there had been something familiar about it. The creature's skin had appeared red, but the face had resembled that of Scorpio.

"It's another of them," he said excitedly, grabbing Misha. "Another *Lesovik!* It went right past me and into the store."

Both of them peered inside. The figure was leaning over the counter menacingly. It had hold of the shopkeeper by the lapels and he seemed to be interrogating him, shaking him slightly at intervals. The shopkeeper wriggled and tried to pull away as if frightened of the thing's strange face.

"We don't need Scorpio. Let's capture this one, and this time we won't put our trust in anyone. We'll exhibit it ourselves."

"How lucky, here's a bag," said Misha, finding on the street corner near a kiosk a canvas sack that had been used to transport newspapers.

"All right. You stand on that side of the door. I'll get its attention as it comes out and you can capture it."

"It looks a little bigger than Scorpio," observed Misha.

"So? We'll just charge more for a look. Quiet now, I think it's coming."

The mysterious figure stepped from the doorway, and Vasha held up a cigar. "Excuse me, *gospodin*, do you have a light?"

Before there was time for a reply, Misha pounced, throwing the sack over the creature's head and securing it around its waist with the cord.

"We have it!" shouted Vasha, a moment before the being swung Misha off his feet. Vasha grabbed it in a bear hug, but was surprised at the rock hardness of the thing's body. He and Misha tried to hang on as the creature careened blindly down the street. The bag muffled its shouts of rage and made them sound like the growling of an animal.

"Help us!" Vasha shouted at a soldier passing by, and he began to move in their direction, along with some factory workers who first pointed and laughed at the spectacle. "Hang on!" he shouted to Misha who was being shaken like a leaf in a high wind. "Help is coming!"

As if he heard this, the being redoubled its efforts to escape. There was a snap as the cord around its waist gave way, freeing its hands. Vasha noticed that it wore something like a thick black bracelet on its wrist, and when it raised its hand a beam of intense light shot out of the device, passing between two workmen and scoring a black line on the pavement. Those who had been coming to help scattered and ran. The creature grasped the sack in both hands and tore itself free. Vasha let go and landed in the dirty slush of the gutter. Misha, his eyes closed, was still hanging on like a bulldog as the creature began to run down the street, but as it rounded the corner Misha was thrown off and fetched up against a lamppost.

Seeing his brother sprawled on the pavement, Vasha cried out in alarm and ran over to him. But as Vasha approached, Misha sat up and grinned, rubbing his head.

"After all, you did ask the creature for a light," he said with a giggle, pointing to the seared line on the pavement.

In the darkness of a Russian dawn, Leah moved through the throngs of workers leaving the textile mill as their shift ended, handing them copies of Radek's latest manifesto. She kept a wary eye out for Blacklegs, for she was now much more aware of the dangers of this activity. She remembered the sad, slow convoy of prisoners on their way to exile in Siberia, and did not want to join them, or meet some more violent fate. She was halffrozen by the time she had looked into a thousand numb faces and had shoved a leaflet into a thousand unprotesting hands.

"A good night's work," said Pugatchev, approaching with what was left of his own packet of leaflets. "Come with me to the café and we'll warm up over a cup of tea. Maybe the gypsies will be singing there."

"No, I've got to go home," said Leah.

"Still mad because I ran off and left you to the police?"

"A little."

"Now that I've gotten to know you, I wouldn't do it again," he said.

She blew on her hands, to warm them. She didn't ever believe a word he said, but it was hard not to like him anyway. She could depend on his directness. When he looked at her or gave her compliments or tried to give her a hug, it was obvious what he wanted. At least his intentions weren't all mixed up with altruism. *Sometimes people who are too complex get on your nerves*, she thought, without naming any names.

"All right," she said, "but I can't stay long."

The café was small and decrepit, but a samovar boiled on the counter, and two gypsies sang the melancholy songs that were so popular here. Pugatchev gave Leah a lump of sugar from his ration and showed her how to drink her tea worker style. One clamped the sugar lump between the teeth and sipped tea through it. It took some practice, though. Leah laughed, dropped the sugar and nearly scalded her chin with boiling tea.

Radek entered as they were laughing together and came to sit at their table. "I'm glad that working for the revolution doesn't get in the way of your social occasions," he said.

"But this is revolutionary business," said Pugatchev with a smirk. "I was just about to invite Leah to come with me to the Socialist meeting this evening."

"She can't, she's busy."

"No, I'm not busy at all," said Leah. "I'd like to go with you. What is it about?"

"A local organization is being formed to promote the idea that the workers should take over the factories and the land should be given to the peasants. Lenin himself may make a brief appearance. And then, of course, after the meeting we would go for a candlelight dinner and discuss the ideas." He reached over and took her hand as he said this.

"I've been thinking of attending this meeting myself," said Radek. "We could all go together—three friends." He said the final words as if he were spitting poison.

Leah wondered how she got into these things. More to the point, how she was supposed to get out of them?

The meeting reminded Leah a lot of the moujiks who had sat before the fire, endlessly discussing the ills of the world. Most of the participants were men: soldiers, workers, peasants by their dress, though there was a sprinkling of dapper men in suits, and a few women. Stale smoke swirled toward the ceiling in the rented hall and the air was full of talk. A flurry of activity and excitement heralded someone who entered and mounted the podium to speak.

"It's Lenin," whispered Pugatchev, his voice filled with awe.

Leah saw a short, stocky man with a big head, bald and bulging, set down in his shoulders. He had little eyes and a snub nose, a wide, generous mouth and heavy chin. She noticed that he wore shabby, wrinkled clothes; his trousers were too long for him and hanging over his shoes. She thought him commonappearing enough and when he began to talk, it was in a voice rasping and husky as if he had worn it out by too many speeches. What he said was straightforward, untouched by whimsy or humor, but the crowd sat enthralled, heads nodding, shoulders beneath greatcoats hunched forward intently. She sensed that he held the attention of the crowd by virtue of his intellect alone. There was substance beneath the lack of style.

He painted a world to come that shocked Leah—a world turned upside down, where the lowest classes supplanted the highest, where the workers ran the factories and the peasants owned the land. No king or pope or central authority would send down pronouncements. *Soviets*, or councils made up of deputies or representatives chosen by the members, were already forming among the lower classes. He spoke of a revolution not just in Russia, but worldwide, where those who toiled threw down their tools to pick up arms and take their rights by force if need be. It was an exciting idea. By the time he had finished speaking, Leah was almost convinced.

Ringing applause broke out at the end of his speech, and then he was whisked away, to whatever other appearance he had scheduled that evening.

The chairman of the meeting, a fierce-looking little man with bristling mustaches, dressed in the kaftan of a peasant, began to preside over the organizational meeting. Leah could follow little of it, and with all the people, the hall was becoming stifling. Leah noticed that Radek seemed restless, too. His eyes glittered as he rose, asking leave to speak.

The chairman recognized him.

"I only wished to ask a question," he said. "As to whether you really believe the workers and peasants are ready to assume control of the factories and farms. As you know, most of them are ignorant, and education—"

"We are not entertaining questions at this time," said the chairman.

"But surely you will hear a dissenting opinion," persisted Radek.

"Lenin's doctrine of Democratic Centralism admits no dissent," said the chairman. "Once the leaders have decided on a course of action, it must be carried out."

"But what if I don't agree—"

The chairman made a gesture and two burly men came up from behind Radek and grabbed his arms. He was hustled from the room to the sound of catcalls from the audience.

Leah's head was pounding from the smoke and lack of air. She decided she'd had enough of the meeting, too. "I think I'd like to go home now," she said to Pugatchev.

"I know, I know, you want to go and commiserate with our friend Radek. But, of course, you're free and can do as you like."

Leah made her way out of the crowded room, stumbling over feet and knees of those in the assembly. Radek was sitting on the front steps, head in hands.

"Did they hurt you?" she asked, sitting beside him.

"Not much," he said. "They tossed me into a snowbank and that broke the fall. They're wrong, and they wouldn't even listen. Their Lenin knows a great deal about organization, but not much about democracy. We're lucky that his is a small group and will probably have little influence when the revolution comes."

With all the revolutionary activity going on, Leah had neglected her regular attempts to contact Scorpio. It seemed that the bond between them had atrophied the more she became involved in events of her own world.

Perhaps it wasn't all that strange. When she had told Radek she needed an identity, it had been the truth in another sense, too. A *human being who leaps through time must be something like the train travelers,* she thought. *It's all too easy to be caught up in movement for its own sake and then to find yourself hurrying to one meaningless destination after another.* To avoid that she had leapt wholeheartedly into Radek's struggle, hungry for human contact and meaningful action.

Since she couldn't make mind-contact, she considered other means of finding Scorpio, but the city was so large, a search could take months. She was discouraged about her chances of ever finding him, but one day her luck changed. When she came into the printshop that morning she found an open newspaper lying on a worktable.

"Who left this here?" she asked, noticing that it was a much different sort of literature than Radek turned out.

"Oh, that trash? It's not mine. I guess it belongs to one of the other tenants." Radek picked up the paper. He began to read articles at random. "'Chaliapin now appearing in the opera Don Quixote. The audience goes wild.' Can you imagine people spending their time reading such drivel when society is in turmoil?"

"I suppose it's not so strange that somewhere people continue to enjoy life," observed Leah.

"'Mme. Sverdlova the well-known theosophist leader introduces her newest discovery, a psychic medium with a very distinctive appearance. According to Mme. Sverdlova his talents rival those of the famous *starets* Grigori Rasputin and we are certain to hear more of this amazing protégé.

"What?" said Leah, sitting there with a stunned look on her face.

"Didn't you hear me? I'm not going to read that drivel over again. Throw the paper away; it's an insult to all thinking beings."

"No, I didn't mean 'what, I didn't hear you.' I just meant—'what.'"

Radek looked at her speculatively. "Have I been working you too hard?"

"No, I'm fine. This psychic you just read about. I think he must be the man I came to Petrograd to find."

"You never mentioned coming here after some man," said Radek.

"He's not exactly a man," said Leah, "but he is a friend and I have to find him. Is there a way to find an address for this Mme. Sverdlova?"

"I suppose I can ask around. If she's in the newspaper, I'm sure she's not a recluse."

Radek soon found Mme. Sverdlova's address, and Leah dipped into her dwindling funds to hire a droshky. Streetcars didn't run through this area of the city where the wealthy lived in homes almost as impressive as palaces. Leah was excited as the droshky pulled up at last before the Sverdlov townhouse. She had almost come to believe that Scorpio was lost to her forever, and now she was remembering their travels together and wanting to see him. Radek rapped at the door and after a few minutes a lanky, black-clothed man appeared. He eyed their garb and said in frosty tones, "Please come around to the servants' entrance in the rear."

"But we're not anybody's servants," said Radek.

"We've come to see someone we believe may be staying here," said Leah, insinuating herself between Radek and the butler. "Do you know of someone called Scorpio? If he's been here, I'm sure you'll remember. His appearance is, well, distinctive."

"Master Scorpio is indeed here, but he has requested that he have no visitors," said Hookes. Actually, it was Mme. Sverdlova who had made that request, in fear that the Mishkin brothers might return to try to get Scorpio back.

Upon saying this, the butler closed the door firmly in their faces. Though Radek pounded on it again, there was no response.

"Maybe you shouldn't do that," said Leah. "They might call the police."

"But they have no right to treat us this way."

"We'll come back. I don't believe Scorpio doesn't want visitors. He knows I'm looking for him."

Chapter Eight

Grigori Rasputin descended the marble steps of an ornate staircase at the Winter Palace. When he reached the bottom, his heavy boots echoed on a polished parquet floor. The immense room was bordered on two sides with alabaster columns whose cornices glittered with gold. A massive chandelier with myriad candle-shaped bulbs blazed overhead. The furnishings were all on a large scale, of polished mahogany decorated with gilt bronze in the fanciful shapes of Greek gods and goddesses and other designs from classical antiquity. Rasputin thought the decorative sphinxes and chimeras employed as table legs and chair armposts were almost sinful, hieing back to pagan times. The palace was not the sort of place Rasputin felt comfortable in, if anyone did. Agreeably enough, the Tsar's family spent as little time as possible in the Winter Palace, though they had to be present from time to time on State occasions.

His idea of comfort was his own dacha, or country home, in Siberia. Despite his duties at court, he still spent a great deal of time there. In his heart, he was still a moujik even though destiny had conspired to make him almost an equal of their Imperial Majesties. He could never tell them of this equality, but he felt it, all the same.

Even though he had risen high, and had much influence, Rasputin looked out of place here. He was sturdily built, of medium height with long greasy black hair and beard. He continued to dress peasant style, except that now his trousers were of blue velvet and his shirt of silk. Around his waist he wore a sash embroidered with blue cornflowers, and his boots were handmade of the finest leathers. But despite this finery, since he had retained his peasant notions of hygiene, he had a pungent, unpleasant smell. His face was broad and placid, with bushy eyebrows over steely gray eyes.

Those eyes set him apart. They were deep-set and could fix upon something or someone with frightening intensity. Ever since he had been a boy, and had been ill, he had been considered different in his village. After his illness, when his father's mare had spooked at a noise and was kicking out the sides of the stall, he had gone in and with soothing words had calmed the frantic beast. He found that this calming effect worked on human beings as well.

He had just sat beside the bed of the Tsarovitch Alexei, his presence and soft words soothing him to sleep. Whenever Alexei became ill, his parents summoned Rasputin, and this was why a peasant had gained access to royalty. Not that Mama and Papa didn't have a great need of his presence and advice. Things were going very bad just now, with the war and the talk of revolution. *But if Papa had just paid attention to my advice to stay out of the war, things wouldn't be in such a state,* he thought. *Well, I must continue to help the Tsarina; she pays attention to my advice, anyway. Especially since I foresaw that Alexei's health would improve in his twelfth year.*

He crossed a wide expanse covered with a Persian carpet and stood before a small white door with a pattern of fleur de lis in gold. The knuckles of his huge hand tapped at it gently.

"Enter."

The Tsarina Alexandra Feodorovna entertained guests in her private sitting room. The room's color scheme was mauve, the Tsarina's favorite color, and gold. *Everything small and dainty, as in a house for dolls,* Rasputin thought. *And even in winter, flowers and ferns everywhere.* Alexandra sat on her mahogany chair with armposts carved in the shapes of swans. *The Tsarina resembles a swan herself,* Rasputin thought. She wore a shy, yet serene expression, a double strand of pink pearls setting off her white throat. Even though she took Rasputin's advice and depended upon him for the care of her son, her presence daunted him, so regal did she appear.

Across from her on a couch sat a lady whom Rasputin didn't recognize. She was tall and sticklike with rusty red hair pulled up in a knot. Her hands fluttered like two pale moths as she talked. Beside her sat a well-dressed man with a muffler hiding half his face. *Only a fool would wear such a thing indoors,* Rasputin thought. It gave him a bad feeling.

"How is Alexei?" asked Alexandra.

"I left him sleeping peacefully, Mama."

The other woman stiffened in her chair at this informal word of address used to greet an empress, but Rasputin didn't care what she thought. She was of little importance and bad to look at, so he attempted to ignore her.

"Mme. Sverdlova, I don't believe you've met Grigori Rasputin, my trusted advisor."

"Charmed," said Mme. Sverdlova in a voice that said she was not.

"And, Grigori, you may have something in common with this gentleman. Scorpio, Mme. Sverdlova's protégé. He's a gifted spirit medium and she tells me he's a healer, like you."

"Few are like me," said Rasputin, and then asked with peasant candor, "Is there something wrong with his face?"

"Not at all," said Mme. Sverdlova, nodding to Scorpio to unwind the muffler.

The Tsarina made a barely audible gasping sound and then regained her royal composure. Rasputin stared unabashedly. He had had dreams and visions, but nothing as strange as this had appeared in them. The creature's eyes were immense. In the dimness of the room they seemed to glow with an inner blue light, like the depths of water. Rasputin shook himself, as if awakening. This was not good.

"Mama, you must not let this one see the Tsarevitch. He would frighten the boy, and I have a bad feeling about him."

"Mme. Sverdlova and I were only taking tea, and talking," said Alexandra smoothly. "I have been so interested in theosophy and spiritualism. I have read so many books, but Mme. Sverdlova and Scorpio are experts in these matters. We have had a very good conversation, that is all."

Rasputin made a sound that was more a growl than a word. "I must go," he muttered.

In the carriage on the way home, Scorpio turned to Mme. Sverdlova. "Do you think Rasputin will find out that I am to see Alexei tomorrow?"

"Oh, no, the Tsarina promised that it would just be our secret. He is an unpleasant man, isn't he?"

Scorpio thought that was somewhat of an understatement. When Rasputin had stared at him with those eyes like hot coals, he had felt the innate violence of the man. Undeniably Rasputin had a kind of crude psychic power, which he probably used to serve his own greedy desires. But Scorpio sensed that encroaching on his territory could be dangerous. Not to mention that without the orb, his session with Alexei tomorrow had little chance of success.

He hated to hold out false hope to a mother whose child was ill, but on the other hand, it would be hard to tell Mme. Sverdlova that he had no powers without the orb. He wondered what could have happened to Leah. He had seen only the side of the city that Mme. Sverdlova knew: the theatres, the fine restaurants, the glittering shops along the Nevsky Prospect; yet he could imagine grimmer surroundings. Even the rich were touched by the growing shortages of food and other goods, and the burgeoning unrest of the masses.

Even though he had repeatedly tried to contact Leah, he'd had little success. Once, he thought he saw a dimly lit café in which someone was singing a sad song. He seemed to see the shapes of two men at a table, but then the image faded. He supposed he could run away, but he had no place to run to.

• • •

"Alexei, this is Scorpio," said Alexandra. "He has come to visit with you this afternoon." This introduction made, she withdrew, leaving Scorpio alone with the Tsarevitch.

Scorpio made the same sort of bow that he had made when meeting Queen Elizabeth. "Your Majesty looks very handsome this afternoon," he said, thinking that royalty demanded these sorts of obvious lies. It was called flattery, and he had been told that kings and queens doted on it. Unfortunately, he wasn't very good at it.

The boy looked small and pale, and much younger than his thirteen years. He wore a military-style suit and a small soldier's cap. Scorpio had been told that Tsar Nicholas was at the German front, so this garb must have made Alexei feel closer to his father.

Sitting near the boy was an immense soldier. Pyotr was Alexei's constant companion, charged with the Tsarevitch's well-being and safety. The man sat by stolidly, as if he were a piece of the furniture. In a sense he was.

Decorated as lavishly as everything else in the palace, Alexei's room had a few touches to show that it belonged to a child: a puppet theatre that rivaled the Mariinsky in its ornateness, a gameboard of inlaid ivory and ebony, a rank of pewter soldiers skirmishing on a marble-topped table.

"You're not human," said Alexei, and then more tentatively, "are you?"

"No, I have to admit that I'm not," said Scorpio, suddenly glad to put pretense aside. The adults had to pretend, for their sanity, that he was a very strange-looking human being. A freak. But of course he knew that there was nothing at all wrong with his looks—he was a handsome specimen of the Aquay. "I'm from another world, actually."

Alexei looked a bit doubtful.

"Terrapin has warm green seas, and my people, the Aquay, are at home in the water. Our castles, built of millions of glistening shells of the domesticated sea-chert, have towers that rise out of the sea. It's a beautiful place, but I don't know if I'll ever see it again." Scorpio gave a sigh.

"You don't like it much here, do you?"

"No. I've met some good friends, but things are very complicated in this world. I just don't belong here."

"As far back as I remember," said Alexei, "I've been sick. If I try to run and play like other children, I injure myself and then I must lie in bed for a long time. Even when my first cousins are brought here to play, they treat me differently because someday I'll be the Tsar. Sometimes I don't like it much here myself. But I suppose we must make the best of it. Do you play chess?"

"No, I'm afraid I don't."

"It's a war game. It's important for a tsar to understand war, you know. But I grew tired of playing it with Pyotr. He always lets me win."

The big soldier smiled shyly. It was the first time he had seemed human to Scorpio.

Alexei went to a bureau and got out a chess set with pieces made of antique silver cast in realistic shapes. For most of the rest of the afternoon, they sat over the chessboard as Alexei taught Scorpio to play. "No," cautioned the boy as Scorpio moved a piece. "The pawns are like foot soldiers; they can move only forward, a square at a time. But the knights, the horsemen, may move in any of four directions, diagonally—so!"

"But what of the king?" asked Scorpio.

"The king moves," said the boy, laughing, "anywhere he wants to!"

They had a congenial time, though Scorpio could do nothing of a healing nature without the orb, and he was certain his charade would be exposed when the Tsarina returned.

After a while they put away the chessboard to go outside, and as they began to descend the long staircase, Alexei looked longingly at the curving marble banister and stroked it with his hand. "As long as I've lived here, I've dreamed of getting on that banister and sliding down to the bottom," he said, "but, of course, he won't let me." Alexei made a gesture toward the soldier who was following close behind. "I asked him to at least do it so I could watch, but he says he's too clumsy and would fall off, and anyway, he would be court-martialed for doing such a thing in the palace."

Scorpio thought a minute. "Look at me," he said.

The boy appeared startled, but did as he said.

"Now concentrate as hard as you can on me, and I'll do the same for you."

Scorpio quickly climbed astride the banister. "Are you concentrating?"

The boy's face was clenched and intent. It didn't seem too likely that this would work, since he didn't have the orb, but it was worth a try since the boy would probably never get to experience this for himself. It was a foolish thing, yet seemed somehow important.

Scorpio let go his hold and began the dizzying descent of the polished surface. He tried to project the sensations of speed and the friction of his clothing against smooth marble. He was concentrating so hard on sending his impressions back to Alexei that he forgot to slow his speed as he neared the bottom. When he reached the end he went flying off. Someone standing at the bottom of the stairs broke his fall and they went rolling together across the parquetry.

When Scorpio looked up, still laughing from the novel experience, he looked into the burning eyes of Rasputin.

"You! Here with the Tsarevitch. Against my advice." Rasputin quickly got to his feet and brushed off his fine clothes. Scorpio saw the capacity for violence in Rasputin's expression and knew he wished to do more than issue a rebuke. In the presence of Alexei and his guardian, he didn't dare. Rasputin made that growling noise again and slunk away, but Scorpio had the feeling he wasn't really giving up.

Alexei had reached the bottom of the stairs. "When you were sliding down, I did feel something ... I think. It made me dizzy but it was exciting. But the best part was when you landed on Grigori."

Scorpio couldn't be sure that mind-contact had really been made, but he knew that sometimes imagination was almost as good as the real thing.

When Alexandra appeared, Alexei ran to her, his eyes shining. "Scorpio and I had a fine time today, Mother. Can he come back soon?"

"Why, you seem in good spirits," said Alexandra. "And I believe there is a little color in your cheeks. How can we repay you?"

Scorpio felt a little flustered that she thought he had done this for money or influence. "I can't take pay for helping people," he said, "and anyway, I enjoyed myself, too."

Rasputin left the palace and returned to his own lavish apartment. For a while he acted like a madman, throwing furniture about the room, smashing crockery, hitting the wall with his fist until there was a bloody smear on the plaster. He saw the influence he had gained slipping out of his grasp.

Finally, he fell across the bed, panting from exhaustion, and after a while achieved a semblance of calm. Rasputin knew a great many people in Petrograd, the high and the low. In his nightly excursions to drink and listen to gypsy music, his passion, he had met some men who would be glad to kill for the price of a few rubles. All he need do was contact one of them ...

He rose, feeling much better. The problem was simple, after all, and he would get in touch with one of these men tomorrow.

Tonight, he had been invited to a party by young Prince Yussupov. At first, he had thought it a bit strange, since the prince, like most of the rest of the members of the Romanov family, were against the influence Rasputin exerted on Mama and Papa. But the prince was an important fellow, and perhaps he was relenting a little, deigning to socialize with a mere peasant.

But I'll show them that I'm more than a peasant who has happened to fall into a lucky situation. His mood had come full circle, and he was feeling very happy as he dressed in his best clothes. *I'm a man of destiny*, he thought, as he surveyed himself in the beveled glass of the mirror. *Like a god. I'm never going to die!*

There was a gentle rapping at his door. Prince Yussupov had come to convey him to the festivities. He felt excited. It was going to be a memorable night.

Chapter Nine

The next day Leah and Radek stood behind a grill work fence just outside Mme. Sverdlova's townhouse. It provided little shelter against the wind, but they were out of sight and they could wait to see if Scorpio left the house.

"This person must be important to you to have us out here shivering in the cold for two hours," complained Radek.

"I told you. He's a friend. And no one said that you had to wait out here."

"I don't want you standing out here alone, and besides, I'm curious. He might not come out, you know."

"He has to. We've waited here every day for three days. Sometime luck has to be on our side."

"Look," said Radek. "Maybe luck *is* with us."

As they watched, a black carriage drawn by two matched dapple gray horses was brought around to the front of the house. It had the Sverdlov crest on the side. Mme. Sverdlova came down the front steps, and right behind her was Scorpio. The two were just getting into the carriage when Leah ran up.

"Leah!" said Scorpio, leaning down out of the carriage to clasp hands with her.

"Who *are* these barbarians?" said Mme. Sverdlova. "Driver, whip up the horses and we'll leave them behind."

Radek grabbed the horses' bridles and at first was nearly swept off his feet as the driver's whip cracked.

Scorpio climbed over the side of the carriage and fell in a heap on the pavement. Radek let go of the bridles and stepped aside and the frightened horses took off down the street at a gallop, Mme. Sverdlova shouting at the driver to stop.

"I'm free!" said Scorpio as the runaway carriage disappeared around a corner.

"Let's get out of here before she finds a policeman," said Radek.

They went to the workers' café they often frequented and found a place at their usual table. Scorpio looked around at the dim, smoky atmosphere, the battered furnishings. "This place is familiar," he said.

"Don't tell me Mme. Sverdlova took you to lunch here," laughed Radek.

"I meant that Leah must have been here before. I know I never have," said Scorpio.

A lean, mustached waiter in a stained apron interrupted their conversation to take their order. His mind didn't seem to be on his business.

"Did you hear the news?" he asked. "Word is out all over the city. Rasputin is dead!"

"Dead?" said Scorpio. "But I saw him and talked to him just yesterday and he seemed in fine health."

The waiter drew his finger under his chin and made a cutting sound. "The mad monk was murdered, or so they say."

"This will stir up the Romanovs' hive," said Radek. "Do you know who did it?"

"No, not really. The stories sounded a little exaggerated. They said that he was poisoned, shot, bludgeoned and finally drowned in the Neva."

"I think any one of those would be enough to finish a mortal man," said Leah.

"Maybe, but I've heard some strange stories about Rasputin," said Radek.

"Some of them were undoubtedly true," said Scorpio, remembering his run-in with Rasputin the day before. He recalled the look Rasputin had given him as he slunk away. Scorpio shivered.

"He had influence over the Tsar, didn't he? What will his death mean?" asked Leah.

"You mean to us? And our work? I would say that Rasputin's death removes an embarrassment to the Empire. But really, all the damage has already been done. The balance has tipped against the Tsar and there is nothing he can do. Those of us who have waited for revolution have only a little longer to wait."

Leah took the fur-wrapped orb from her handbag and passed it surreptitiously to Scorpio who held it beneath the table and peeled back the wrappings.

"You kept it safe for me."

"I made certain it was always kept warm."

Radek looked at the two of them in puzzlement as golden light seeped through a crack in the wooden tabletop.

"I tried to make contact with you, but I couldn't because that woman kept me so busy," said Scorpio.

"You don't look as if you've suffered too much," said Leah, looking at Scorpio's fine suit and fur-collared coat. She laughed at his spats. Aquay ankles tended to be skinny and the feet large in proportion.

"You don't know how many operas and ballets I've sat through," said Scorpio. "And the tea parties. It was excruciating. But, I did learn one thing of importance. There is, in the city, a scientist who is working on a theory of space and time, a Professor Mirskaya. I repeatedly asked Mme. Sverdlova to allow me to visit her, but she always had an excuse."

"Well, of course I know about Professor Mirskaya," said Radek, as if glad he could contribute to the conversation. "She was teaching at the University when I was taking classes there."

"I must meet her," said Scorpio. "I've been seeking someone with her knowledge over the past several centuries—that is, for a very long time."

"I did not know her well, and I'm not sure she would remember me, but I know where she lives. At least we can try."

They were kept waiting at the door of Professor Mirskaya's building for some time in the buffeting wind, but at last a small peephole opened. They could see only a blinking eye, but when they made their request a sepulchral voice said, "The professor is very busy and has asked that she not be disturbed."

"I am a friend of Professor Mirskaya's from the University," insisted Radek, jingling a handful of coins as if in idleness, "and I'm sure she will want to see us."

The door opened and a *dvornik* blinked out at them. He had a pale, soft look, and his eyes were red-rimmed and watery.

"Perhaps she would," said the *dvornik*, reaching out casually for the money with a pale, puffy hand. He opened the door wider to admit them. His smile showed that he had no teeth, only white, bloodless gums. "Zavgorodny is not the kind of man to keep friends apart." He looked intently at Scorpio, who was wearing his muffler wound around his face again.

"Zavgorodny is the kind of man who would do anything for a kopek," said Leah when they had gotten out of earshot. "I'm glad he's not the *dvornik* at my building. I'd fear to come home at night."

When they knocked, Professor Mirskaya opened the door a crack and stared out at them with a vaguely surprised look.

She was an angular woman wearing a man's faded bathrobe, a single house slipper and a pencil stuck into her disheveled light brown hair.

"I'm sorry," she said with a distracted air. "I don't know you people. I cannot be disturbed when I'm working." She seemed about to close the door again.

"We met at the University, I believe," said Radek. "David Levovitch Brodsky. Don't you remember?"

"No, frankly, I do not. I left strict orders with Zavgorodny that I was not to be disturbed; therefore, you paid him money face. Gray skin and those big staring eyes!

Later, when Police Sergeant Leontiev made his usual visit, Zavgorodny was trembling with excitement, his white flesh quaking.

"You asked me to keep an eye on the scientist who once worked with a German," he said.

"Yes," said Leontiev. "We're keeping watch on all potential German sympathizers."

"I saw something today. Someone very strange went in to see the professor. I don't think he was exactly human."

"Perhaps you've been buying too much vodka with the money I give you," laughed Leontiev.

"I saw him. I swear it. Isn't it true that the Germans are devils, that they are working on all sorts of diabolical weapons of war?"

"They're already using gas against our boys, so I'm sure they would stop at nothing. But do not let your imagination run wild, Zavgorodny. Just do what I pay you for. Keep watch and report what happens."

"That is what I mean to do," said the *dvornik*, smiling his grotesque toothless smile. "Exactly what I mean to do."

Scorpio sat nervously in Mirskaya's apartment a few days later. He was eager to get to work, yet afraid that he would have yet another disappointment. He had not yet found anyone who could help him learn to control the orb. Perhaps it was asking too much of a human being to understand something so alien.

He remembered earlier sessions. Mirskaya had brought in a large chalkboard and had filled most of it with equations. When she had turned from her work, he saw that her sweater was buttoned wrong and she wore the same distracted look he had seen that first day when they interrupted her.

"Now, Scorpio, consider these equations a sort of time map," she had said. "Pay attention as I take you through it." That had begun several long, difficult sessions, where he strained to understand her theory. It was even harder in that he knew he would be trying to actually apply it.

When she had finished, Scorpio had a better grasp of how time worked, though he wasn't sure he had followed her on every point.

"We're going to try a short hop first," she had said, once the mathematical studies were behind them. "How about five minutes into the past."

"That doesn't sound so hard," Scorpio had said, grasping the orb firmly and attempting to use the coordinates the professor had given him.

Scorpio had opened his eyes, expecting to hear Mirskaya repeat her words about the equations on the chalkboard, since that was what had been going on five minutes ago. But she only sat looking at him expectantly. He hadn't jumped at all, even though he'd tried. "It didn't work."

Mirskaya had taken notes busily for a moment and then asked him to try to go back into last week. No luck on that either.

Several more sessions had proved no more fruitful.

"This is frustrating," said Scorpio at last. "The orb has never failed me before."

"But from what you've told me, you've always taken big jumps before. I wonder if there's not some sort of Ubiquity Effect here."

"Ubiquity Effect?"

"If you had gone five minutes into the past, you would have met yourself in time, doing whatever it was you were doing five minutes ago. If you went a week into the past, there might still be the chance that you would meet yourself, if you were in the same general area."

"But that's silly. I'm only one being. How could I possibly meet myself."

"That's just the problem. As human, and ... other beings, we have our limitations. I'm not sure that we're ready to accept the idea of meeting our former selves in time. Maybe the orb knows that, and for the sake of your sanity, it won't let you be in two places at the same time."

"Are you ready to try?" asked Mirskaya. Scorpio was drawn out of his thoughts. Since they had had no luck with the short hops through time, and since a long jump seemed extremely risky given the short time he'd been working on this, they had decided that he should try moving through space and only a few seconds forward in time.

"I think so. I've begun to think of time as a chessboard. You know, the pawns, ordinary folk, can go forward in time or space only the usual way, but with the orb, I'm like the knight. I can move diagonally, so to speak, and do not have to cross intervening terrain in order to get where I'm going."

"That's a good analogy," said the professor. "It should help you visualize what you must do."

"Where should I try to go?" asked Scorpio.

"Preferably to a place you've been to before, so that it's easier to concentrate on."

“What about the Finland Station?” asked Scorpio. “I came through there when I arrived, and it’s quite large and spacious, in case I have trouble navigating.”

“Too public,” said Mirskaya. “It would cause a riot if you just appeared out of nowhere.”

“I didn’t think of that. Of course you’re right. I might try to go back to Mme. Sverdlova’s townhouse. She knows me, and she and her associates often experiment with the occult. My appearance would only be taken as that of an astral body or some such.”

“A private home should be all right,” said Mirskaya. “And since you spent some time there, it should be a good subject. Try to visualize a room in the house. Concentrate deeply.”

Scorpio began to concentrate, though nagging memories of his stay with Mme. Sverdlova kept intruding. He recalled her domineering ways and insistence on his attendance at social functions. He felt the skin of the orb forming around him. It was too late to change destination now. He was being swept away by the power of the orb.

Chapter Ten

Leah awoke to the sounds of shouting. It was as if someone was going up and down the halls, pounding at the doors. She wondered for a moment what was going on. Then she heard a splintering crash, and someone's scream.

Galvanized into action, she leapt from bed and dressed quickly. Peering out a window she saw several police trucks and what seemed like a crowd of uniformed men. As she watched, Mr. and Mrs. Zahadin from downstairs were being taken out in manacles and loaded into the truck.

She heard more shouts, loud footsteps coming in the direction of her apartment, and she knew she couldn't stay here. Opening the door a crack, she peered out into the corridor. So far it was clear. How long did she have? Taking a chance, she darted for the elevator. It was empty; evidently Katya had heard the police and had made her escape by the stairs.

She had become less frightened of the elevator than when she had first come, and she had watched Katya operating it, but she wasn't sure she could do it herself. Grasping the levers, she pulled one and the elevator lurched and wheezed, moving upward. Correcting herself, she pulled the other and the elevator began to descend with a jerky motion.

When she reached the ground floor, she saw an immense policeman through the bars. He had an ugly pockmarked face and a sledgehammer in his hands. Frantically she jerked on the lever to keep the elevator descending past the floor. His face red with rage, the policeman gave the elevator a whack with his hammer as it passed him by. The whole cage shook, and Leah was afraid it might come loose and send her crashing to the basement. But once past the floor it resumed its gradual descent. Then the elevator was shivering and clanking to a stop in the basement.

"Radek!" she shouted as the elevator stopped. "The police are here. They're arresting everyone!" Quickly she threw open the doors and joined him.

"We have to get out of here," he said, turning toward the stairs.

"They're all over the ground floor."

Radek eyed the ramp and the double doors at the end of it.

"No. That won't work either," Leah told him. "They're outside the building, too. I imagine they've surrounded it by now. We can hide. Come on. Over here."

Pugatchev had covered the motor car with a piece of canvas. Leah lifted the cover and they crawled inside, letting the canvas drop back. It didn't seem likely the police would overlook this hiding place for long, but there wasn't anywhere else to go.

"Stefan said the motor car was almost completed," whispered Radek. "He told me he was going to try a test run today. Too bad he won't get the chance now."

Leah made a gesture to silence him as she heard heavy footsteps on the stairs.

"Say, what have we here?" said a voice. "This must be their printing press."

"I told you this was where all those seditious leaflets were coming from. Bring the hammer, Lieutenant."

"No," said Radek so loudly that Leah was afraid the police would surely hear. "Not my press."

She threw her arms around him, sure that he was about to climb out of the car and take on the police with his bare hands. Her tactics worked, for he settled back into the seat. The ringing sound of hammer smashing against metal brought him bolt upright again, and she didn't think she could hold him back as he heard the police laughing as they worked.

"Did you say Stefan was ready to test this thing today?" whispered Leah. "That means that maybe it'll run."

"It also means that maybe it won't."

"Can you make it work?"

"I think so."

"Then now's the time, while they're having so much fun destroying the printing press."

"All right. I guess we have to go down trying. Like Nechayev." He crawled from the car. Leah hoped the police wouldn't look in their direction. She wasn't sure what he was doing, but she had seen Pugatchev use a metal crank at the front of the thing, as if it were wound up, like a mechanical toy.

The police were making a great deal of noise now. Several hammers were ringing against metal and the first coughing sounds of the engine as it attempted to start went unnoticed. But then the motor came to life with a full-throated roar, and Radek threw back the canvas and jumped into the driver's seat.

Leah had been half afraid it wouldn't start, but now that it did, she was even more terrified as the machine roared and shook, its parts clanking together with an awful racket.

The police were shouting and pointing and running in their direction. Only one of them picked up a rifle. Leah saw him aiming as the car began its ascent of the ramp.

"I wish we had had a chance to open those doors!" shouted Radek over the noise of the engine. "This wasn't Stefan's idea of how to launch it!"

The policeman's rifle went off, loud in the enclosed space. Leah heard a whine and then a crack as the bullet smashed into the doors ahead of them. She could no longer see the policemen; she had ducked down in the seat and had her hands over her head.

There was a sudden impact, throwing her forward, and an awful splintering of wood. When she looked, the car had stuck halfway through the doors.

Radek was cursing and grinding the gears. Suddenly the motor car shot backward at great speed. Leah looked over her shoulder and saw policemen scrambling to get out of the way. Two of them disappeared beneath the car.

Leah saw the policeman with the rifle now take careful aim. It didn't seem possible that he would miss a second time. She saw a shimmer of gold in front of the rifleman. The orb-craft was appearing out of nowhere. She recognized Scorpio's shape limned within it. *How did he get here*? she wondered. *I thought he had no control over the orb.*

As the orb appeared directly in front of the rifleman, he looked startled and his shot went wild, ricocheting off the ceiling.

Here we go!" said Radek, who had noticed nothing. He started the motor car forward again, taking another run at the doors.

When Leah looked back, the orb-craft was just winking out of existence, as if Scorpio had found this location too dangerous and had lifted off again. *But where did he go?* she wondered. *Has he just gone on to some other world—without me?* She wasn't sure if she were sorry about it or not, but she did feel a sense of loss.

Before she could think much more about it, the car smashed through the splintered doors out into the street, where it nearly ran down a policeman and his captive.

Radek hit the brakes as Leah recognized Pugatchev. "Get in!" he shouted. Pugatchev pulled free from the startled policeman and ran for the car, having just enough time to leap aboard it as Radek put the car in motion again. Leah helped to pull him inside as Radek swerved back toward the policeman, laughing as the man staggered out of the way and fell into the mud and slush of the gutter.

"It runs!" shouted Radek over the engine noise. They sped away down a side street, the car's rubber tires bouncing over the cobblestones.

"I knew it would!" Pugatchev shouted back.

Leah hid her eyes, and a moment later peered through her fingers to see scenery going by in a blur. This was worse than the train. She felt the force of their acceleration and the wind whipping her hair.

"Radek, stop!" she shouted, hiding her eyes again. "We're going faster than people were meant to!"

"Yes, we're going fast," Radek agreed, evidently not hearing what she said. "We're speeding along at almost thirty miles an hour. They'll never catch us now!"

Scorpio appeared in Professor Mirskaya's flat. There was a sharp popping sound as the orb bubble burst, dropping him unceremoniously upon her floor.

"You came back!" she said, as if there had been some doubt in her mind. "Are you all right?"

Scorpio sat up, moving his legs and arms to see if they still worked. "I had to come back fast," he said. "I wasn't sure where I was at first, then I saw it was the basement of Leah's apartment house."

"Not exactly according to plan."

"Maybe my telepathic link with. Leah made me miscalculate, or I just didn't want to go back to life with Mme. Sverdlova. Anyway, the police were there. They had smashed the press and they were chasing Leah and Radek, who escaped in a vehicle."

Professor Mirskaya looked doubtful. "Do you think the orb might induce dreams?" she asked.

"No, it was real."

"But you managed to get back here."

"Not directly. I was confused and in orb space for quite a while. Of course, it doesn't seem as if I was gone that long, but—"

"Perhaps time as we know it doesn't exist in orb space," said the professor, pausing to jot something in her notebook.

"I can't worry about the orb now. I have to get back there and see if they escaped, or if there's anything I can do to help."

"Of course. And if you need a place to stay for now, you can come back here. I think we're making great progress and I'm eager to continue."

Scorpio gave her a vague answer and went out.

• • •

Zavgorodny stood behind the small peephole he had made in the professor's wall, rubbing his small, red-rimmed eyes. He had seen the professor alone in the room, studying over notes, and then suddenly the alien creature had been there. Not as one goes in and out by a door, but one moment not there, and poof, there he stood. The sergeant thought he was crazy when he talked of German superweapons, but did this not prove that he was right?

Zavgorodny imagined himself standing behind a podium at a great gathering, and the sergeant was pinning a medal to his breast. "I only did it for my country," he would say, and the crowd would break out in applause for this hero who had saved them all.

He stopped and shook his head, and amended that scenario to have the sergeant presenting him with a bag of rubles. After all, one could not eat medals, and the yammering of the crowd was only so much noise. He would not wait for the sergeant's visit today; he would go over to his office and report these developments at once.

After the motor car had taken them many versts away from the apartment house, Radek slowed its speed and finally pulled it over to the side of the road. He slumped over the wheel, thinking of all the people the police had captured. What would happen to them? They could be sent to a work camp in Siberia, or worse. The presence of the printing press would undoubtedly make things harder for them.

He knew what the revolutionary catechism had to say about the situation: that the revolutionary had no real allegiance or responsibility to anyone, only to his cause. But he wasn't worthy of the catechism because he couldn't help feeling a certain guilt and responsibility. After all, he knew these people, had worked shoulder to shoulder with them. In his fervor he hadn't honestly thought about the practical consequences of their actions, and now he had escaped and his followers were left to pay the price of his recklessness.

Though he thought first of his comrades, he couldn't help feeling a certain sickness in the pit of his stomach about the printing press. It had been a thing of power, disseminating words of freedom to all the oppressed. Now it was a pile of scrap. The voice of their cause had been silenced.

For a long time there was no sound, except for the occasional metallic ping of the cooling engine. At last Radek looked up at Leah and Pugatchev. The struggle between his ideals and his conscience showed on his face as he said, "Comrades, we have failed, totally, in what we tried to do. I'm sorry I put both of you in danger."

"N'chevo," said Pugatchev without rancor. "I think it might be wise to split up, in case they're still on our trail. You know where to find me, if I'm needed."

Radek nodded. Pugatchev jumped out of the car and disappeared down an alley. Radek wasn't worried about him. He could take refuge with his Socialist friends.

"We put ourselves in danger," said Leah. "If you're taking all the responsibility for what happened on your own shoulders, don't. Give the rest of us a little credit."

"I should have known," he said, "that words are not enough. Words are never enough when you're dealing with oppressors and murderers. I knew this was a struggle, but I didn't fully understand that it was open warfare. You can only meet violence with violence."

"We can't dwell on the unfairness of it," said Leah, "we have to be concerned with practical matters. We must find a place to stay, and that may not be so easy. Word will be out with our descriptions, so if we go to the house of a relative or friend, they may be put in danger."

"Yes, I must find you a safe place to stay," said Radek. "Then I have business, important business to tend to."

"Oh, no. You're not going to leave me off like excess baggage. Didn't you call me *tovarish*? Didn't that mean anything?"

Radek looked at her and felt pulled in two directions. What he was thinking about doing was potentially suicidal. He wanted her well out of the way of it; yet, she was right. Women couldn't be equal unless they also shared the danger.

And then, of course, there was the revolutionary catechism. He had to steel himself against the weakness of caring for someone so much that it got in the way of his mission. He had thought every part of the catechism glorious before; it hadn't occurred to him that trying to live up to it could cause so much pain and confusion.

"All right," he said. "You may go with me, since you're determined. But you may not care for some of the people I'll be working with. And what I must do may not be to your liking."

He was right. Leah felt very uneasy when Radek met his new comrades in the café. Smirnov, the one she considered the leader, wore a black patch over one eye. A ropy scar came out from beneath the patch and curved down his whiskered cheek. He had two companions, but she could not say which was the more grimy and furtive-looking.

She had made the choice to come with Radek because she had sensed his mood and was afraid of what he had planned. She wasn't sure she could make any difference, but she didn't want to let him go off on his own. She sat sipping tea through the sugar lump clenched in her teeth and listened to their talk.

"Earlier when we tried to recruit you, you told us that violence was old-fashioned," said Smirnov. Leah couldn't tell whether he sneered when he talked or if it was the scar lifting a corner of his lip. She decided it was a little of both. "We thought you were going to save the world with your manifestos and pronouncements."

"I can't do that now, can I?" said Radek. "After the police made my press into borsht."

Smirnov and the others laughed. "It didn't take you long to learn how things really are. We can provide the explosives, and the plan. If you've really got the guts to go through with it."

"I'll go through with it. What's the plan?"

Smirnov took out a short-bladed knife and proceeded to cut a map into the soft wooden surface of the table. "Here's Tsarskoe Selo, the Tsar's retreat. And here's the track connecting it with Petrograd. You mine the tracks here and place the detonator up here on the hill. That way you can see the train coming and be sure of your quarry."

Leah felt a shock as the man began to talk about explosives. She had had a feeling that Radek's plan had something to do with violence, but she hadn't thought about them involving bombs. There was so much chance of an accident, especially as they were inexperienced with explosives.

"The Tsar has been at the front," continued Smirnov, "but he comes back at intervals to see his family, and they are often at Tsarskoe Selo together. We'll meet tomorrow and familiarize you with the equipment."

When they had gone, Leah sat in silence, staring at the lines on the tabletop.

"Well, then, say it," said Radek.

"You're crazy," said Leah. "You don't know anything about explosives, foul weather has made the roads impassable, and if the imperial coach travels along this route, it's almost certainly guarded in some way. You'll never manage to kill the Tsar. You'll only be needlessly sacrificing yourself and whoever goes with you."

"That seems to be the plan," said Radek, "but no one said you had to be a part of it."

"I wouldn't miss it for anything," said Leah.

Several days later Leah and Radek were driving down a country road in a haze of snow. The road itself was only a faint track beneath the fresh snowfall, and Leah didn't know how long the car would be able to labor through these drifts. She looked at Radek, his face set and implacable, his hands clenched on the wheel. It seemed that only a madman would be out in this storm on such a mission. Yet she hoped to convince him that while violence might be an answer for people like Smirnov, it wasn't his answer, or the way to make things better. Violence was only a downward spiral, a leveling process that finally made equals of men and beasts. Or so her father had taught her, and she had nothing more to cling to than those beliefs, now centuries old.

The dynamite Smirnov had given them was in a crate in the back seat, carefully wrapped in felt padding, the detonating device beside it. Their mission had an air of unreality about it, enhanced by the drifting veils of snow. Leah was actually counting on the snow; once the car was mired in a drift, they could no longer continue their journey, and Radek could be persuaded to return to Petrograd.

Suddenly Leah felt the car lurch and heard the roar of a laboring engine and the scream of slipping tires. What she hoped for had happened. The car was stuck in a snowdrift.

"Well, I suppose we'll be forced to go back now," said Leah.

Radek gunned the motor, rocking the car forward and back to try to drive it clear of the drift. "Nonsense. Here, you slip behind the wheel, and I'll show you what to do."

"Me, drive this demon chariot? No! I couldn't."

It took a few minutes, but Radek eventually convinced her, and with Leah in place, he jumped out of the car and began to push. She screamed and threw up her hands as the car moved, and Radek had to come back into the car to talk to her patiently again.

After a few tries the car broke clear of the drift with Leah more or less in control. She held the wheel stiffly, terrified that the car would careen off the road. It only crept, coughing and sputtering, to a halt.

"If you want it to keep moving, you must keep your foot on the accelerator," said Radek, catching up to her. "Get out and I'll show you how to crank it."

Feeling that she knew more than she wanted to about the workings of the motor car, Leah was relieved when Radek took his place behind the wheel. She couldn't help feeling that this mechanical device was something evil. It had no right to move under its own power. Trains and streetcars were bad enough, but there was something arrogant about an individual encased in metal with so much power in his hands. The results could only be bad.

Twice more the car bogged down in snow. Leah was forced to steer out under Radek's direction, learning more each time and becoming slightly more comfortable in control of the car.

When they reached their destination, Radek parked the car on a hillside. Below them, they could see the railroad tracks. Radek shouldered the crate and told her to get the detonator.

"Be careful with that," she warned. "You know you don't know anything about explosives."

"I know what I need to know," he said, floundering through the snow down the hillside. Leah followed at a distance, holding her breath every time he almost stumbled and fell.

Radek used a small shovel to dig out a space beneath the tracks. He connected the detonator and placed the bomb in the hole he'd dug. Then he covered his work with fresh snow.

"Do you understand that you're not playing a game," said Leah. "That you mean to take a man's life? How will you feel afterward?"

"I'm not about to destroy a man," argued Radek as he played out the wire, burying it in the snow. "I'm sweeping away the debris of history." He found a rocky ledge about halfway up the steep hill, where he set up the detonator. "We can oversee everything from here."

"Not if it keeps snowing. If it snows any harder than this, you won't know when the train reaches the bomb."

"I'll know it somehow. It'll be a glorious sight when the coach and everyone in it is blown to bits!"

"Perhaps there has been a change in plan and Smirnov isn't right about the Tsar's journey. We'll just sit here for nothing."

"I'll sit here until my hand freezes to the plunger," said Radek.

While they waited, the snow lessened and finally stopped altogether. With Radek becoming more and more a stranger, Leah began to wonder why she had come on this fool's errand.

Radek jumped up, pointing. Leah saw a smudge of smoke on the horizon. Then the train came into view, its mechanism vaguely insectile, like a laboring column of ants. As it drew nearer, Leah saw the imperial coach, painted a bright blue.

"It's the Tsar," gloated Radek. "Now he'll pay for his crimes."

Leah watched in horror as the train came closer. It didn't seem possible that she was taking part in this. Now she would have to watch helplessly as the train went up in a burst of fire and smoke.

Chapter Eleven

Scorpio spent the week after the police raid trying to find a lead as to where Leah had gone. There were armed sentries around the perimeter of her apartment building, and he didn't dare approach them because they would certainly ask to see his papers, and he had none. He roamed the Vyborg district, describing Leah and asking passersby if they had seen her. No one had.

Finally he remembered the workers' café where she and her friends had sometimes gathered. It was early in the morning when he went there, and it was almost deserted. There was only the mustached waiter with the greasy apron, and he was sweeping out the place. Scorpio described Leah to him and asked if he had seen her.

"It may be that I've seen such a one recently," said the waiter, pulling on the ends of his mustache, "but my memory is bad."

Scorpio took out his wallet. He had been in this society long enough to know what was needed. He had pawned the golden pocket watch and cufflinks Mme. Sverdlova had given him.

"Ah, now it comes back to me," said the waiter as Scorpio counted rubles out on a scarred tabletop. "I know the one she was meeting with, and he comes in from time to time, but I do not know if you want to deal with him. He is a hard man with a bad reputation."

Scorpio counted out several more coins.

"But I will arrange a meeting, for this afternoon, if you wish it. He may know the whereabouts of the one you seek."

Scorpio left, thinking that he may well have paid money for nothing, but this was the only lead he could find. On his way back to the professor's apartment, he began thinking about the Tsarevitch, and how the game of chess had helped him to visualize movement with the orb. When he had been there before, he could do little to improve the boy's condition, other than to cheer him up a little. Out of their mutual alienation they had formed a bond of sorts. Now that he had the orb, there was no reason that he couldn't go back and restore the boy's health. It would be a pleasure to see him running about the gardens or sliding down the imperial banisters.

As he approached the guard at the gatehouse, Scorpio turned down his coat collar and removed his hat, so the man could see his face. He had been there twice before with Mme. Sverdlova, and the man certainly could not forget *this* face. "You will remember me," said Scorpio. "I was here before for a healing session with the Tsarevitch and he was much improved. If you convey the message that I've come back to complete the treatment, I'm sure that I'll be admitted."

"I do remember you, *gospodin,*" said the guard politely. "You must have made quite an impression because the Tsarevitch has personally told all the soldiers on guard that you are to be admitted should you return. However, today it is impossible—"

In a reflex action, Scorpio reached for his wallet, but the man continued.

"—because the Tsarina and her children have left for a journey to Tsarskoe Selo. They are to meet the Tsar who has gone there before them in secret. If you wish to return later they may be in residence here again."

Disappointed, Scorpio turned away, a vague unease nagging at him, the feeling that time was slipping away. He wondered why he should be concerned if the royal family wanted to take a trip. He remembered the boy's unhappy expression as he told about his illness and wished that he had been here so that he could do something about it. *Well, perhaps later*, he thought, and proceeded toward the café, where he had an appointment of sorts.

Scorpio hadn't sat at his table long before a roughlooking individual slouched in. He had a black patch over his eye and a scar that twisted the corner of his mouth upward. Scorpio felt nervous as Smirnov came to sit down at his table. *Leah can't be dealing with this sort*, he thought. *Maybe this one has carried her away and wants a ransom.*

In the dim light, Smirnov leaned forward and stared at Scorpio. "I didn't think I would ever see a man as ugly as me, but I believe you're even uglier—*tovarish*," he said with a coarse laugh, slapping Scorpio roughly on the back. "This puts me in a good mood. Buy me a drink, and I'll see if I can remember this woman you're seeking." It took several vodkas, but eventually Smirnov was ready to talk. "I don't know if you're a police spy or not, but even if you are, it'll do you little good. Too late to get there now. This Leah you talk about has gone with Radek to carry out a mission of great importance. I don't believe either of them will come back, but that's a small price to pay for the elimination of a thorn in our sides. I honor them for their bravery." Smirnov lifted his glass in a maudlin toast.

"Why do you call them brave? What is this mysterious mission?" asked Scorpio, feeling that sense of unease again, of time ticking away.

"They have gone to blow up the imperial coach as it travels to Tsarskoe Selo."

"Leah? No, you're lying. She would never do such a thing!"

"Maybe not, but she seemed eager enough to follow along with Radek when he made his plans, and they did not seem finicky about the shedding of a little blood. A true woman of the revolution. Maybe this is not the one you are seeking after all."

"But I don't understand. Why would they want to attack an innocent woman and her children?"

"They are to attack the Tsar, you idiot, not women and children!" He banged his glass on the table. "More vodka, more vodka!"

Scorpio gestured toward the waiter to fill Smirnov's glass a final time and then he left.

Pondering what he had been told, Scorpio hailed a droshky and had himself driven to a nearby park. He needed a place to think. Smirnov could have been lying, but the nagging sense of doom that had been dogging him all day wouldn't let him believe that. He had known the people Leah had fallen in with had been doing some dangerous things, printing forbidden literature and the like, but he didn't think they would do anything foolhardy or suicidal. A mistake had been made. Radek thought the coach would contain the Tsar, but it contained the royal family instead. If it were possible to let them know—

He took out the orb and stared at it. I might be able to use this to reach Leah, he thought, but I also might end up anywhere at all and I don't even know where she is. Time is running out. I'll have to try to get the message through.

He became immobile on the park bench in the thin gray light of a February afternoon and sent his message questing toward Leah.

Leah had exhausted her arguments and she stood silently watching the train come closer. Something was seeping into her consciousness. She strained after it and it disappeared, but when she sat down and let her thoughts run free, it returned.

She could see Scorpio's long-fingered gray hands cupping the orb. *Why would he expose the orb to the cold?* she wondered. *He knows what effect it can have.* It was obvious that only a matter of importance would make him risk the orb. She was inwardly silent, concentrating.

She saw the blue imperial coach standing still at a railroad station, and someone was getting on board it. She saw a woman in an ermine-trimmed coat shepherding several children before her. Four attractive girls and a young boy in a military-style uniform. But she didn't know who these people were.

She tried to send back her confusion and the link was lost momentarily. As if it were in another world, she saw the train approaching, Radek's intent gaze, his hands ready on the plunger.

Then she made the connection. Not the Tsar boarding the train, a family, the Tsar's family. The Tsar is not on board.

She had almost shouted the message as it thundered into her head, but she bit her lip, knowing that she couldn't tell Radek what had just happened. He'd never believe it, and to shout it out would give him a warning.

The train had nearly reached the spot where they'd planted the dynamite. In another moment Radek would be pushing the plunger down. She could see him tensing for the action. There wasn't much time to think. In a more chivalrous age, she could have fallen upon her knees and asked him to spare the train in the name of love, but she had been here long enough to know that wouldn't work. Finally deciding, she threw herself at him with all her strength.

Taken by surprise, Radek was knocked sideways. He let go of the detonator, which toppled off the rocky ledge. It rolled down the hillside for a few feet before becoming buried in a snowbank. Leah held her breath as she watched it. The wrong movement would detonate the bomb. But nothing occurred and the train, blowing its whistle jauntily, passed by.

Leah turned in time to see Radek, his face an awful mask of rage, stalk forward to confront her, or perhaps worse. She had to admit he wasn't himself, and hadn't been since the raid on the apartment house. She had called him crazy as a challenge, but maybe he really was. Who knew what he would do?

He never reached her. There were several loud reports and Leah was sprayed with snow. Radek went down with a scream and to Leah's horror she saw that the side of his thigh had been torn away in a gaping bloody wound, and blood was jetting out onto the snow.

At first Leah didn't know where the rifle shots had come from. Radek tried to rise and fell back. "Cossacks," he said. A troop of riders in long coats with bandoliers over their shoulders and large fur hats came riding full tilt up the shoulder of the hill. One stopped to fire again, and she threw herself down near Radek. Cautiously, she crawled over to him and took off her scarf to wrap around his leg above the wound. She wound it tight with a stick, staunching the flow of blood for the moment.

"We have to get out of here; they'll dismount and climb up after us."

"Dismount? You don't know much about Cossacks."

"I don't know anything, and I don't think I want to." As she watched, the riders at the front of the troop didn't slow their mounts even when the hill rose in a steep rocky slope. A horse slid sideways; another fell backward almost crushing his rider. One of them almost made it, and Leah was frozen to the spot, almost ready to cheer the feat. A rock-slide began beneath the horse's hooves, making it struggle frantically to try to keep its feet. Finally it lost its balance and tossed its rider, both of them rolling down the slope.

Seeing what had happened to their comrades, the other Cossacks reined in their horses. Some of them went to tend to the fallen and the others shouted and gestured, deciding on another route to the top that the horses could negotiate more easily.

"Come on," she said, attempting to draw Radek to his feet.

"Leave me," he said. "You might make it back to the car without me. It's your duty, as a proper revolutionary, to sacrifice me."

"You're the proper revolutionary, not me," said Leah, helping him to rise. With Leah supporting Radek, they staggered toward the car, leaving a trail of his blood, a clear track in the snow.

She heard the clatter of hooves on stone not far off as they reached the car. She shoved Radek inside, still complaining that she had not left him as she ought to have done. And now she was behind the wheel.

She heard gunfire and saw snow fly up as the bullets struck. They were still out of range.

"You have to turn the crank to start the engine," said Radek, who by this time must have decided he didn't really want to be sacrificed.

Leah had forgotten. She jumped out of the car and awkwardly inserted the crank in the aperture in front. She turned it with all her strength. The motor gave a thunderous cough as it struggled to start in the cold air, then it began to roar loudly.

"I did it!" she shrieked, jumping behind the wheel and trying to remember all that Radek had told her earlier. She got the car in motion just as the Cossacks found their range and a bullet slammed into a tree beside them.

The car fishtailed on packed snow, but she managed to keep the vehicle on the road. The horsemen didn't give up. Every time there was a bend in the road, their horses cut across, and they managed to stay right behind Leah and Radek.

Leah remembered the places where the car had been stuck before and hoped that the trail they had broken through hadn't been covered by drifting snow. Radek had fallen sideways in the seat, unconscious, so this was her problem alone.

A straightaway gave her an advantage, and she floored the accelerator, trying not to think of the harm such speed could do to the human body. When she looked back, she saw that her lead was growing. The motor car might be monstrous, but it had one clear advantage over the horse: it didn't get tired.

Radek awoke the next morning in a warm bed in the cheap hotel where he and Leah had taken rooms temporarily. Snow was drifting past the windows in a typical sort of morning in Piter. He sat up, feeling like someone who has suffered a long illness, but awakens to find the fever broken. When he moved, he felt a sudden pain. Looking down, he saw a crude bandage of torn sheets on his thigh.

Leah came into the room with a bundle of newspapers under her arm. She stopped, evidently surprised to find him awake. By her expression, she was unsure of her welcome.

"I remember being shot" said Radek, "but not too much after that. Did you take me to a doctor?"

"I'm a doctor. Well, sort of. The bullet tore through the flesh without touching the bone. I cleaned the wound, and dressed it. I believe you'll be all right, but I've contacted

Scorpio and asked him to meet us here. He'll complete the healing process."

"I thought he was some kind of fake faith healer."

"His healing powers are real enough, although they're not exactly his."

"Who drove the car?"

"Who do you think?"

"After you threw your hands in the air and screamed? It must be a miracle that we got here."

"Not a miracle, but certainly very lucky," said Leah. "Are you still angry that I kept you from completing your mission?"

"I'm too weak to be angry now," he said, falling back onto the pillow. "I'm not sure. Something happened to me after the police raid. I was so carried away with my own revolutionary zeal I hadn't realized anything could go wrong. Still, you've changed history, you know, by stopping me from killing the Tsar."

Leah was silent a moment as if considering what it might mean to change the course of history. "No, the Tsar wasn't on the train," she said finally. "It was his family going to Tsarskoe Selo to meet him. We would have killed a woman and her children."

"I don't know how you could know that, but if it's true, killing them would have been a great blunder. The newspapers would have used it to evoke sympathy for the Tsar. Killing the innocent never serves a just cause."

Leah looked at him and smiled. "I thought you'd like to see the latest news," she said, handing him the stack of papers. He grew more jubilant with each paper he opened, the headlines reading, "Strike in the Vyborg: Thousands of Workers Leave Their Jobs" and "Riots Break Out. Women March in the Streets, Demanding Bread."

There was a tap at the door and Leah went to admit Scorpio. They looked at each other uncomfortably for a moment, and then they joined hands, only briefly. Radek could swear that there was some bond between Leah and this strange-looking man that he would never understand. Scorpio took out the small, shining globe Radek had only glimpsed before. He walked over to the bed and applied the thing to Radek's wound.

"This could take a few applications, if the wound is deep," said Scorpio.

"It is," said Leah.

Radik felt a sensation of warmth and well-being begin to grow as the orb touched him. Pain drained out of his leg, and then the wound began to itch intolerably, exactly as if it were healing at a prodigious rate.

Chapter Twelve

The Hunters dropped out of orb space near the Sverdlov townhouse. More than one willing informant had told them that Scorpio had been staying here, or at least the informants had been willing with Ardon's hands on their throats.

The very proper Hookes met them at the door. "I'm sorry," he said, "Mme. Sverdlova is seeing no one today." His composure seemed only a bit shaken by the tall figures that stood before him, muffled in crude garments of hide and fur.

"She will see us," growled Ardon, picking up the butler and whirling him over his head before tossing him into a snowbank. They entered the house, oblivious of the screaming maids who scattered before them.

Finally, they collared a servant and asked where they would find Mme. Sverdlova. The man pointed a shaking finger at a green baize door. Lethor leaned close to the door, listening. He heard weird noises: the sounds of trumpets and drums, snippets of high-pitched, otherworldly music. He supposed there was some sort of sound-making device hidden in the room. Then a high-pitched female voice intoned, "I call upon Punjabi, my spirit guide. O Spirit, come from the astral realms and speak."

As Lethor swung the door open and entered with Ardon right behind him, he saw several females gathered around a small table. An oil lamp cast shifting light on their intent faces. "I'm looking for Mme. Sverdlova," he said.

For a moment those at the table were silent because of the otherworldly quality of Lethor's voice.

"I'm Mme. Sverdlova," someone stammered. Lethor located the light switch and pushed it.

The crystal chandelier suddenly blazed with hundreds of tiny electric flames. Those at the table began whispering to each other nervously. "But who are you, and how did you get in here?" A tall, thin female in elaborate, flowing garments rose as if she would confront him.

As Lethor took off his hat in the warm room, the other females saw his face. Several of them shrieked in fear. Chairs fell back with a clatter as they leapt from their places and bolted for the door. Lethor let them go. Mme. Sverdlova gaped at Lethor. "You're like him#x2014;like Scorpio. Well, not exactly, but—"

"It's Scorpio we seek," he said, putting himself between her and the door when she attempted to dodge past him. "We know he was here. Don't lie to us, or—"

"I have no intention of lying," said Mme. Sverdlova in a small, tightly controlled voice, as if she were trying to retain the last shreds of her dignity. "At least not where that ingrate Scorpio is concerned. I did everything for him, took him everywhere, introduced him to the best people, and what did I get in return—"

"Where is he?" demanded Lethor.

"Well, I'm sure I haven't made it a point to find out, when he ran away from me with those awful people."

Lethor moved threateningly, and she began to speak faster.

"I did hear later, however, that he was working closely with that traitorous scientist Mirskaya, the one who worked with the German. Scorpio always did seem interested in her for some reason." Mme. Sverdlova's voice became a squeak and seemed to stick in her throat.

"Tell us where this scientist lives and we will go," said Lethor.

Mme. Sverdlova obliged, though her face was now pale and doughy-looking, as if she were close to fainting. Lethor casually moved away from the door. Her eyes darting about like those of a trapped animal, Mme. Sverdlova made her escape.

"So, after all his travels, Scorpio has found a scientist," said Lethor. "He must believe he can learn to control the orb."

"He doesn't have a chance," said Ardon. "He's only prey, after all."

"I'd like to think so, old companion," said Lethor. "But from what we've seen in this world, primitive though it may seem to us, it looks as if Scorpio has at least a chance of learning something useful. We must reach this scientist quickly and remove her."

As Lethor began to activate the orb, its light dimmed and gave off a sickly greenish glow. "What's wrong with this thing? I wonder," he said, shaking it until the healthy golden aura returned.

"It was very cold in that abandoned warehouse where we spent the night," said Ardon. "Maybe it is affected by too much cold. I know that my toes haven't been warm from the time I arrived here."

"Don't talk nonsense. Something as transcendent as the orb can't be affected by a mundane cause like adverse climate, no matter how much we may suffer from it."

"But I think—"

"You know very well that Betas are not bred to think."

Ardon touched his forehead in the Beta gesture of obeisance.

When he should have been on duty, Zavgorodny was taking a nap in his room. He was disturbed by the sound of the bell being rung insistently, over and over. He shuffled to the door and looked out through the peephole.

"Have a little patience, *gospodin,"* he said peevishly. "Give a man a chance to get a little sleep."

"We have come seeking Mirskaya," said a voice that made the hair rise on the back of Zavgorodny's neck. It was low-pitched with a rasping, monotonous sound. If bees in a hive had a voice, thought Zavgorodny, it would sound like that. The voice made him curious about the visitor's face, but a fur hat pulled low shadowed the man's features. Another figure bulked large behind the first visitor. Two of them. And very suspicious-looking, Zavgorodny thought.

"She is not here," said the *dvornik.* That wasn't true, but he didn't intend to open the door, and he hoped the lie would get rid of them, at least until he could summon the police. There was something frightening about those two in their crudely made fur garments.

"We are willing to wait," said the visitor.

"Not that long. I meant to say that Professor Mirskaya died yesterday. Very sad."

The two outside put their heads together in a whispered conference. *Who cares if they don't believe me?* thought Zavgorodny, feeling safe behind his thick oaken door. *What can they do?*

They had not gone away, but he couldn't see what they were doing. As he leaned against the door, he smelled smoke. He suddenly felt very warm. A hissing red beam shot through the door, and he jumped back with a shout. *How can this be?* Zavgorodny thought desperately as the beam cut a neat charred circle around the lock, an occasional flame leaping up and trying to catch in the wood. *It must be the superweapon! First they burn the door and then*—The lock fell inward right at Zavgorodny's feet. He felt as if he were going to faint as two bulky forms entered.

"We seek the dwelling of Mirskaya," said that inhuman, buzzing voice. Despite the hat, Zavgorodny caught a glimpse of bright red skin, large staring eyes and a beaklike structure in place of a mouth.

"Number seven," Zavgorodny said in a quavering voice. "She is in number seven." He fell to his knees, locked his hands together and began to beg for his life, expecting at any moment to hear the sizzle of the red death ray. He had shut his eyes so it was several minutes before he ceased to whine and plead.

At last he opened his eyes and got to his feet. The apparitions were gone. For a moment he stood there, rubbing his eyes and trying to decide if they had been real, or a hallucination. The charred door caught his attention, faint wisps of smoke still spiraling upward. They were real enough. It now occurred to him where he had seen a face like this before—Scorpio.

The Germans are creating an army of monsters with flame weapons with which to overrun us, he thought. I must tell the sergeant at once!

He had the presence of mind to grab the door lock as evidence. No one would believe this otherwise. Then he ran out into the street, forgetting his coat and hat. He hurried along; unused to such exertions, his soft flesh jiggled and his breath rasped loudly in his throat. It was probably a miracle that he reached the police station at all. Idling policemen exchanged amused looks as Zavgorodny rushed in shouting for Sergeant Leontiev.

"Here I am," said Leontiev, peering around the door of his office. "What's gotten into you, man. You look like you've seen a devil."

"Two of them," panted Zavgorodny, collapsing into a wooden chair that creaked dangerously under his weight. "Remember what I told you earlier about the Germans' diabolical experiments, and that strange creature I saw going into the professor's flat?"

"How could I forget?" said the sergeant.

"I don't think you took me seriously," said Zavgorodny, "but here, look at this." He shoved the burnt section of door into the policeman's face.

The sergeant took hold of it gingerly and studied it a moment. "It looks burned through," he said, "but neatly. A blowtorch might do that, but it would incinerate the wood. I believe there might be something in what you say, Zavgorodny. Did you say the creatures were there now?"

Lethor hammered on the door of Mirskaya's apartment. He wondered if it was possible that what the doorkeeper had said was correct about the scientist being dead. If she were, that would be a lucky thing for Lethor, and for her, as well.

The Hunter chuckled coldly under his breath. He had something that corresponded remotely to a sense of humor, though it was slanted toward the morbid and the cruel. He had decided he would have to burn through this door as well, if only to verify what the doorkeeper had said, when the door was opened and a female indigene peered out.

"Are you the scientist Mirskaya?" he asked.

"Yes, but who are you?" She was staring at them interestedly and after a moment she opened the door, inviting them in.

"May I see you, without the hats?" asked the professor.

"I suppose so," said Lethor, who removed his hat and gestured for Ardon to follow suit. The professor looked in awe at their alien features and at the protuberances on their skulls that looked like coiled ram's horns.

"My, you are handsome specimens," said the professor.

Ardon preened a little at her open admiration.

"Scorpio must have sent you," she said, sounding pleased. "I do see somewhat of a resemblance. Three alien beings. I will certainly be busy devising experiments for all of you."

"Have you and Scorpio been experimenting with a device like this?" asked Ardon, bringing out the orb.

"Yes, exactly like that," said the professor. "We'll make even faster progress with a second one."

Lethor lay the orb down casually on the nearby windowsill. "How far have you come in your experiments?" he asked, wanting to know the extent of the damage that had already been done.

"Well," she said, "we have just begun, but I'm pleased so far. Scorpio is beginning to get a feel for maneuvering the orb through space and time. He has moved through space, though he didn't quite reach his destination. He did come back, though. And I have filled him in on the background of my theory."

"But he hasn't yet mastered the orb completely?" asked Ardon.

"I'm afraid that will only happen in future experiments," said the professor.

Lethor was cheered that so little had been accomplished. "I'm afraid there will be no future experiments," he said, lifting his hand and pointing the wrist weapon at the scientist.

"What do you mean?" She suddenly seemed to understand the menace of the gesture, even though she was unfamiliar with the weapon. "Aren't you friends of Scorpio's?"

"We have come to your pitiful world on the pressing business of killing this Scorpio," said Lethor. "No one would come here by choice. The climate is terrible."

Before he could press the firing stud, there was a loud crash. Several men, using a small log as a battering ram, came crashing into the room.

Ardon heard the voice of the doorman. "There they are! Just as I told you!" and more men were rushing in, their uniforms marking them as some sort of peacekeepers of this barbaric city.

"Try to capture them," said an authoritative voice. "We must find out what these Germans are up to."

A policeman in the forefront had drawn a pistol. "I arrest you in the name of the Tsar," he said, though his voice was shaky.

Ardon lunged toward him with a growl. The policeman backpedaled and sent a bullet crashing into the ceiling. Lethor reached for the orb, noticing for the first time that the window had been left open a crack. The orb felt cold when he closed his hand around it. "Ardon, we must get out of here," he said. The Beta grasped the orb with him, but when Lethor gave the command to jump, the orb light flickered and died.

"What's the matter with it?" asked Lethor, trying to shake it back into life, but it looked withered and dead. "Here they come again, Ardon. Burn them!"

Lethor's beam seared an approaching policeman's sleeve. The man ran about frantically, screaming and beating at the flames. Ardor's shot was better, hitting a man dead center with a vicious sizzling sound. He went down, a curl of smoke rising from his body. As Lethor watched, more men poured into the room. *In these close quarters we'll be overrun before we can burn down all these enemies*, he thought. "Follow me!" he shouted to Ardon, and dived for the window. Shattering glass couldn't hurt his hard skin, but the window was well above the ground, and he landed with jarring force. Somehow he got to his feet and began to run. He was so sure Ardon was behind him, he didn't bother to look back.

When Ardon saw his leader move toward the window, his first thought was to follow. But he saw that two policemen were rushing forward, and they were almost close enough to grab Lethor. Ardon knew his first duty was to save his leader. It was impossible to bring down both enemies with one beam from his weapon, so he had dived toward them, blocking their path with his body. With joy he heard the window shatter as Lethor crashed through it.

Though he had stopped these two, others came running. Ardon felt the jolt as one of them struck him with a rifle butt, but his skull was hard. He got up and was dizzily trying to get his beam weapon into play when several more of them jumped him, bringing him to the floor. They began to kick and punch him.

"Here now. That's enough," said the authoritative voice, from what seemed a long distance away. Ardon drifted into unconsciousness.

The convoy of prisoners, bound for the Fortress of St. Peter and St. Paul, crossed the Troitsky Bridge. They moved slowly, weighed down by their manacles. Eager guards prodded them now and again.

Zavgorodny had begun the journey with an unending stream of explanations as to why he didn't belong here. "I was an informant for Sergeant Leontiev," he had said. "It was I who exposed this vile plot. Just ask the sergeant and he will explain everything."

"The sergeant is beyond explanations," said the guard, grim-lipped. "He was killed in the struggle."

When Zavgorodny had begun to plead again, the guard threatened him with a bayonet. *It will be all right,* he told himself at intervals. *I will explain everything, and then I will be released.* He didn't like to think that his dealings with Sergeant Leontiev had been done for the most part in secret.

Now that the man was dead, there was no one to tell of his part in all this. When the officer in charge had cleared up the shambles in the apartment, he had simply arrested everyone present who wasn't a policeman.

Zavgorodny looked at his fellow prisoners. The alien being was quite placid when he had awakened to find himself manacled, as if he saw the situation and accepted it. The professor tried to look innocent. She didn't seem to grasp that consorting with the enemy in wartime was a serious charge.

They passed through a great barred gate, engraved with the double-headed eagle of the Romanovs. Once inside, he saw what looked like a small, provincial town with streets and shops: a village for the guards, he decided. There was a bleakness about the place, unlike other towns. Only a few people wandered the drab streets, and an all-pervading silence lay over everything.

They passed by an elegant church. Zavgorodny knew that the tombs of the tsars were inside. Above the church rose the spire of gold surmounted by a golden angel that he had often seen from across the river.

"Where are we being taken?" asked the professor, who had not spoken until now.

"To the Alexis Ravelin," said the guard as if taken unawares by the question. "But all who come here must be silent," he added, again gesturing with his bayonet to enforce his orders.

Zavgorodny's stomach knotted. The Alexis Ravelin was the place where the Tsar's greatest enemies were imprisoned. Once in those cells, there was no hope of release. *How can this be happening to me?* Zavgorodny wondered.

The Alexis Ravelin lay beyond a moat, at a little distance from the other buildings. Zavgorodny saw a low-roofed triangular building set amid a few dead trees and uncut clumps of grass. It looked so rustic and commonplace, it might have been a cattle shed. It didn't measure up to the tales he had heard.

None of the prisoners attempted to talk once they entered the Alexis Ravelin. Silence hung heavy here. It was not a peaceful silence, but one fraught with anxiety, as if waiting eternally for the next syllable to be spoken.

Zavgorodny found himself ushered into a small cell. The wall within continued the curve of the vaulted corridor, and the floors and walls glistened with condensed moisture. Spiders had been busy in the corners. Their webs fluttered weakly in a chill draft. The single small, high window had been painted over to leave the cell in perpetual dimness. There was a metal bed and table, bolted down to the floor. An oil lamp, contained in a niche, gave out a flickering glow. The niche was barred, so the prisoner could not reach the lamp. Zavgorodny wondered about it, and then decided it was so a prisoner could not commit suicide by setting fire to himself. Thinking of this with horror, he sat on the bed, his arms wrapped around his bloated body. He had heard terrible stories of the things done in the Fortress, and now all of them came back to haunt him.

Ardon, on the other hand, walked about his cell with great interest. His near-vision took in the view from the window, which consisted only of the skeletal branches of a dead tree seen through a small clear spot in the obscured glass.

This is not a nice place, he decided, *recoiling from the wet slime coating the walls. The gathering dampness was already making his skin feel uncomfortably tight. I will not be here long. Lethor is smart. He will soon have the orb in working order and he will come after me. Then we will settle with Scorpio and his human companion for all the suffering we have gone through.*

Zavgorodny lost count of the days. It was easy to do in this place where the only sounds were far-off and the light of day never penetrated. He noticed that the guards spoke seldom and wore felt boots while walking their rounds. All of the stories he'd ever heard about the Fortress involved violence and torture; it seemed ironic that the most agonizing torture of this place was simple silence.

The unbolting of his door sounded unbelievably loud. Zavgorodny scuttled back into the corner, terrified.

"Come with me," the guard said in a monotone.

Zavgorodny accompanied the guard, trying not to hope that by some miracle the authorities had found out that his part in this had been innocent. But it was hard not to have hope.

Used only to the dimness in his cell, his eyes burned and watered as he was brought out into the sunlight. The guard led him to a large stone building, into a comfortably appointed office. He saw that Professor Mirskaya had been brought here, too. She stood before a chalkboard, pointing now and again to the chicken scratches written there.

A large desk dominated the room and sitting behind it beneath an immense portrait of Nicholas II was a military man with very erect bearing and a monocle. Zavgorodny supposed he must be the commander of the Fortress. His hopes soared. At last he could explain things. He started forward, but the guard restrained him. It seemed he would have to wait for his turn to speak.

In the middle of the desk was the beam weapon that had been taken from the wrist of the alien captive, just a black circle like a thick bracelet of some shiny, seamless material. The commander looked at it from time to time as the professor talked.

"—And that is my theory," she said, finishing what must have been a long and confusing speech, to judge from the commander's face. "The presence of these aliens helps to confirm my theory, since I have postulated the possibility of other continuums. They are visitors who have used the orb, their energy device, to move between worlds and—"

The commander ran his hands through graying hair. "I do not know," he said. "I have seen the prisoner you speak of, and there is certainly something *different* about him. Visitors from other worlds? What a thing to contemplate. Are the Germans inhuman, to bring down upon us such monstrosities as that 'thing' in cell number eight?" He looked up at Zavgorodny. "Who is this?"

"He is the *dvornik* at the professor's building, sir," said the guard. "He had some involvement in the matter, but we are not sure what."

Zavgorodny fell down upon his knees on the commander's Persian carpet. "Oh, please, sir. Nobody will listen to me. I was only defending my country and earning a little money at the same time. Is that such a great crime?" He continued on in this vein until his voice became a practically incoherent babble, so eager was he to tell his story.

The commander made a gesture and the guard told Zavgorodny to be silent, punctuating the order with the tip of his bayonet. "He is of no use in straightening out this mess, and listening to her"—he indicated the professor—"makes my poor head ache."

"Begging your pardon, sir," said the guard, "but of course you know of the unrest in the city. I wonder if it could be connected somehow with this nefarious plot by the Germans."

"Perhaps so. But a decision will have to be made soon on the prisoner in number eight. Take these two back to their cells and out of my sight."

Zavgorodny howled and hung on to the furniture as he was hauled out.

The day after the police raid, Scorpio returned to the professor's building, eager to continue his experiments. He saw several guards posted around the structure and again was afraid to approach. Instead, he waited outside until one of the tenants came out, a short, portly man with a pince-nez and a goatee. The professor had earlier pointed him out to Scorpio as a neighbor and a colleague at the University. The man was forced to show his papers to the authorities before leaving, so Scorpio stepped back into an alley and waited. When he heard the man's footsteps, Scorpio moved forward a little, but not far enough to be out of the alley's shadows.

"Professor Dubrov?" said Scorpio.

Hearing his name, the man stopped and peered nervously into the alley. Scorpio saw him glance back toward the guards, as if for protection.

"I'm a friend of Professor Mirskaya," said Scorpio, hoping that the professor had been on good terms with her neighbor. "I came here today to see her, but there were armed men all about."

"If you're who you say you are, come out where I can see you," said Dubrov.

"I think I'm more comfortable here. I want to help the professor, but I can't if I don't find out what happened to her."

Scorpio saw Dubrov again look over his shoulder at the guards. Their presence was evidently reassuring, and he spoke again. "I would like to help her, too," said Dubrov. "She was always a good neighbor and a fine instructor, but even good people can get involved in bad situations. I warned her not to talk too much about that Einstein fellow. She was very proud to have worked with him, but he is a German, after all."

"And innocent people can be mistaken for guilty," said Scorpio, "especially here. Don't you agree?"

"Yes, I suppose so. I heard that Professor Mirskaya was arrested and taken to Peter and Paul." He spoke very quickly, as if wanting to help, but still nervous that Scorpio hadn't showed himself.

"But what did she do?"

"That I couldn't say. I was told it had something to do with a German superweapon. I *hope* she really wasn't working on such a thing."

"You can take my word," said Scorpio. "She was not. Thanks, Professor."

The man hurried on. He seemed anxious not to be connected with the faceless presence in the alley.

Scorpio took out the orb and was bathed in its radiance. He was glad that Dubrov wasn't here to see this. He'd be sure that the Germans were unleashing a secret weapon.

Scorpio felt nervous about trying to use the orb without the professor's calm voice giving him advice about what to do. *It's my fault that she's in prison,* he thought. *So I have to at least try to get her out.* He began to concentrate, and a moment later saw the cobblestones of the alley grow indistinct through the rippling shell of the orb as it encompassed him.

As the orb came into existence again, he felt somewhat off-balance, as if things were not right. He looked around and saw an immense room whose vaulted ceiling was intricate with designs of gold and bore several beautiful paintings. The wall he faced was of white marble with columns of green malachite. Two colossal and blazing chandeliers illuminated row upon row of glittering mosaics of saints and angels and holy personages. As he turned, he saw a white-robed priest looking at him in alarm.

"Wrong place," muttered Scorpio, and ordered the orb to try again.

Ardon studied the lines he'd made on the wall with a sliver of stone. Four. It had been four whole days and nights, and Lethor had not appeared. Ardon's faith in his leader could not be shaken, but counting the lines gave him a slight feeling of anxiety.

He heard a rattling sound at the door and someone pushed a plate and cup through a narrow opening. He gobbled the slab of black bread and tossed the water into a corner that was growing decidedly more damp. He supposed they continued giving him this poison liquid so that in a weak moment he might consume it.

He lay back on the bed that was much too small for him and focused his near-vision on the small window. If he worked very hard, he could imagine that he saw a glimpse of the sky over his own desert world. His powers of imagination were not great, but the silence of this place helped him concentrate. In his own world there was a carrion bird called a *creaugh* that could retract its head and neck into its body when it flew. It seemed to Ardon that he could see those wide black wings and headless body now soaring in the sky near his cell, although of course he knew that was impossible. In his own country the *creaugh* was a bird of ill luck, and to see one hovering near meant death.

Chapter Thirteen

From her hotel-room window Leah could see that the morning of March 11, 1917 had broken bright and cold. A fresh fall of snow glittered brilliantly in the sunshine. The streets were deceptively quiet.

For days there had been unrest in the city, scattered outbreaks of violence here or there, clashes between protesters and police, but there was nothing to make her think this day would be any different from the one before it.

Someone tapped at her door, and when she opened it, she saw Radek, bringing a parcel. She invited him in, and he unwrapped the package, showing her a small length of sausage and some black bread.

"We'd better enjoy this," said Radek. "I stood in line for hours to get it. There was all kinds of talk in the queues. The people want an end to the corruption of the autocracy." Radek's eyes shone with excitement. He walked now with only a slight stiffness from his wound.

They shared the food without conversation, looking down at the street where only a few figures were stirring. Radek pointed at a convoy of military trucks going on some mysterious errand. After they had eaten, they decided to go out. There was a suppressed excitement in the city that could be felt, if not explained. As they walked, someone came running up from behind them, catching first Leah and then Radek in a friendly embrace.

"Pugatchev!" said Radek. "Where did you disappear to?"

"I had to lie low," he said with a grin. "Last night the police were picking up known followers of Lenin. I kept moving and evaded them. Something is making them very nervous."

Reaching the Nevsky Prospect, they continued to stroll, noticing that jubilant crowds were beginning to form. Some of the people carried red banners, the wind rippling their slogans: "Down with the Tsar" and "All Power to the Soviets."

At around noon they joined a large, casual crowd that had gathered in Znamenskaya Square near the Nikolayevky railroad station. Wherever the crowd eddied, speakers, standing atop trucks or the pediment of monuments, shouted out messages, but no one really seemed to be listening. Instead the crowd was curious and alert, waiting to see what would happen. The square was in a strategic position, commanding the whole length of the Nevsky Prospect.

As Leah and her friends watched, a detachment of troops marched into the square, and the commanding officer began shouting, telling the crowd to disperse, saying that if necessary he would order his men to fire. He received catcalls and jeers for his trouble. Someone threw a rock. "Maybe we should move on," whispered Leah, sensing a recklessness in the crowd that had begun to frighten her.

"They're only bluffing," said Pugatchev, raising his own voice along with others. *"Doloi, doloi!"* he shouted. "Down with him!"

Leah jumped at the sound of gunfire, and those around them jostled each other, several people losing their nerve and running. After a moment everyone realized that the soldiers had fired their weapons harmlessly into the air.

"The army is with us," someone shouted. "All power to the Soviets!"

There were several more volleys, all fired into the air, since the soldiers seemed loath to fire on their own people, and the crowd became more jubilant and rowdy. Leah could not imagine what was going to happen. So far it looked like a standoff. In the next moment she heard the rattle of machine-gun fire and screams. The crowd swirled around her; she found herself separated from her friends and almost pushed to the ground. Though pummeled from both sides, somehow she kept her feet, following the flow of people who ran in a mad stampede.

It was like a nightmare, running with little hope of escape, and knowing that if she fell, the pounding feet of those behind would crush her. Reaching a low stone wall, she scrambled over it, scraping knees and elbows, and found herself in the courtyard of a neighboring house, for the moment, safe from the panicked crowd.

She searched the faces of those around her, looking for Radek. It was impossible to find him in the mob. When the crowds thinned out a little, she tried to make her way back to the square, but Cossacks rode along the perimeter and she didn't dare approach. An ambulance roared past, siren screaming, evidently carrying away some of the wounded.

"Leah!" Radek came running to catch up with her. He looked flushed and almost happy, despite what they had just been through.

"You're all right?" said Leah. "I saw the ambulance. What happened?" She buried her face in Radek's shoulder and let the tears come.

"The officers turned a machine gun on the crowd. Some of our men were killed."

"People were running in every direction. If I hadn't gotten behind a wall, I would have been trampled."

"It's all right now, we're together," he said, holding her for only a moment. She soon got the idea that his mind was on other things. "Did you see the soldiers firing? They pointed their weapons in the air, even when their officers ordered them to fire on us. Something's up. Something big!"

"All the more reason we should go back to the hotel," said Leah. "These streets are dangerous."

"Did you see Stefan?" asked Radek, ignoring her caution.

"No, I lost him in the crowd."

They searched for Pugatchev and finally found him in a nearby tavern, bragging to the patrons of his bravery in the face of gunfire.

Radek couldn't be convinced to take shelter in the hotel, so Leah stayed with him. At four o'clock they passed by the square again out of curiosity, but it looked as if nothing had occurred there. Fresh snow had been shoveled over the blood, and passengers from the train station still walked about, hailing droshkies.

"Just like on Decembrists' Square," said Radek bitterly. "They think they can just cover their crimes with a little fresh snow. But not this time. Not this time. I'm sure of it!"

Though they wandered about the city for what seemed hours to Leah, they didn't see any other signs of violence, though they were told of mounted patrols breaking up small crowds with gunfire and snipers firing from roofs. By the time they returned to the hotel, Leah was convinced that nothing more would occur.

"In the morning, I'll awake and things will be just the same," she told herself, as she escaped from Radek and Pugatchev's eternal talk of revolution and found refuge in her own room. She went at once to her bed. After all, she thought sleepily, pulling the covers over her head, whoever heard of society turning upside down, peasants as kings and kings as peasants? The poor and downtrodden had existed forever in that state and all the good wishes in the world couldn't change it.

Radek's dream of a better society had been only a nice fantasy. She hoped he wouldn't be too disappointed.

She awoke with a start to gunfire and shouts. Remembering the raid on the apartment building, she leapt from bed and reached for her clothes. Only when she was ready to escape did she creep to the window and peer out.

Mobs of soldiers were running through the streets, firing in the air and shouting. She saw men run from doorways and join them. A car crammed with soldiers careened around a corner. Long red banners had been tied to their bayonets and streamed out behind them.

Leah supposed she should be terrified, but all the activity had the air of a drunken carnival. If the army were attacking, they were using a new and strange strategy, every man doing as he pleased.

After a moment she realized someone had been pounding on her door for some time. Radek didn't look as if he'd slept all night; his hair was tousled and his eyes red-rimmed.

"We've done it!" he shouted. "Early this morning the soldiers who took part in the shooting on the Znamenskaya Square held a secret meeting and voted to mutiny. They shot the commander who ordered them to fire on their own people, and went out urging other regiments to join them. Look, look out the window and you can see the result. The whole army is joining the revolution!"

Leah looked out again and saw, down the block, flames leaping from a building beneath a pall of smoke, the occupants swarming out onto the pavement. "They've set fire to the police station," said Radek.

Leah felt the same sense of unreality that came when the orb dropped her into some unexplored world. Peasants were becoming kings as she watched. And the kings—well, she supposed that this moment wasn't such a good time to be a king, or a king's man.

Finally, after a few more mistakes, Scorpio materialized outside a triangular building that looked tranquil and rustic. He felt certain he was in the wrong place again. But then he noticed guards pacing about. *This has to be it,* he thought. Since he had no way of knowing where the professor was being held, he had to go, via the orb, from cell to cell. Appearing from nowhere, he would invariably startle a cell's occupant. But by the time a prisoner had screamed or shouted for help, he was gone again. He had visited quite a few cells in this way before he saw the professor sitting on her cot with her head in her hands.

The orb dissolved silently, leaving him standing there. He cleared his throat and she looked up. At first she looked startled at his presence, then she understood.

"Scorpio!" she said, rushing up to him. "How wonderful! You used the orb to come directly here."

"Well, sort of." He looked around the tiny chamber and noted the masses of spiderwebs, the scuttling insects and glistening slime of the walls. "This is a depressing place. I hope your guard didn't see my arrival."

"There's a sort of peephole over there where they spy on prisoners without being seen. I discovered it earlier when I gave the cell a thorough inspection. I can't say for sure we're not being observed now, but there must have been some sort of upheaval. I heard shouts and running feet in the corridors and the guards are supposed to maintain silence when they make their rounds. It's all part of the atmosphere."

"I suppose we should go," said Scorpio, "in case a guard happens to be watching." "I hope you don't mind traveling with me. I had a little trouble navigating earlier."

"I don't care if we end up on the bottom of the Neva," said the professor. "Anyplace but here!"

He held out the orb and she grasped it with him. Her desire to be out of this place gave speed to their departure, but put Scorpio off-balance again. He had decided to deliver the professor to her office in the University, but when they landed, he saw they were in a small room with shabby furniture. A young woman stood looking out the window. A moment later he recognized Leah.

"Scorpio, Professor Mirskaya," said Leah as she turned from the window.

"My connection to you keeps sweeping me off course," said Scorpio, "but it doesn't matter. I only wanted a safe place to deliver the professor."

"Why should you have to deliver her anywhere?" asked Leah.

"She was in the Fortress, and all because of me, I think," explained Scorpio.

"Not precisely," said the professor. "It was the other aliens. The red ones, with horns on their heads."

Scorpio and Leah exchanged looks, knowing exactly who the professor was describing.

"They had some sort of death ray," continued Mirskaya. "And the authorities thought I had something to do with developing it. The one they captured either couldn't or wouldn't tell them that I had nothing to do with it."

"They actually captured one of the Hunters?" asked Leah.

"Yes, but it took a lot of policemen," said Mirskaya. "Once they got the thing into the Fortress, I'm not sure they knew what to do with him. And then there was some disturbance."

"It's the revolution," said Leah. "The whole city's in a turmoil. This morning the soldiers mutinied, and now they're taking over the city."

"Ah, I see," said the professor.

"Didn't you hear what I said, Scorpio?" said Leah. "The soldiers and the people, peasants and workers, are taking over the city. Have you ever heard of such a thing?"

Scorpio remained silent, as if considering some inner puzzle. At last he said, "I have to go back."

"Back to the prison?" asked Mirskaya.

"Oh, no," said Leah. "No, you can't help them. They've chased us across the universe and would have killed us without a thought. You don't have any responsibility to them."

"You didn't see that place," said Scorpio. "You didn't smell the stink of the river seeping through the walls and floor. The Hunters are desert folk, open-air dwellers. Can you imagine what it must be like to live in such a tiny, dark place?"

"Let his companion rescue him," said Leah. "He has an orb, too."

"Yes, they had a device like yours," said Mirskaya, "but its fire went out, and they couldn't use it."

Scorpio nodded, remembering what had happened to their own orb. It comforted him to think that there would be no immediate pursuit, but he still felt responsible for the Hunter being in the prison. "I can take him anywhere at all," he said. "Even to Siberia. I'll leave him in a small village, like Tutalsk."

"It still makes no sense to me," said Leah, "but you don't need my permission."

Scorpio grasped the orb and leapt back toward the prison. It was easier this second time. Now knowing of the unrest in Petrograd, it was understandable that the place was in chaos. This prison that housed the political prisoners of the Tsar would surely be one of the first targets of the revolutionaries. He moved in and out of several cells very quickly, but didn't see the familiar shape of a Hunter. As he materialized at the corner of branching corridors, he heard voices and stopped to listen.

"Sasha, got a cigarette?"

"You know we're not supposed to smoke on duty."

"What does it matter now. The mobs are massing on the Troitsky Bridge. Old Fish-eye, the commander, fled hours ago, a rat leaving a sinking ship."

There was silence; Scorpio guessed the men lit their cigarettes and puffed away companionably.

"Let's not stand here before cell eight," said Sasha. "It gives me a bad feeling. Did you see what sort of monster they had confined here?"

"I heard, but thought it was just talk."

"No, it was here all right. Its presence had the officers very nervous."

The voices grew more faint as the two men moved farther down the corridor. Scorpio risked being seen in order to hear the rest of their conversation.

"So, if it's not there, then what happened to it."

"The officers solved the problem just like you'd think. They dispatched the embarrassment in cell eight by firing squad just before dawn."

Scorpio wasted no further time, but returned directly to Leah's hotel room.

"You're getting very good at this," said the professor.

"Practice makes it easier," said Scorpio.

"Well, was he grateful?" asked Leah.

"I was too late," said Scorpio. "The soldiers murdered him."

Chapter Fourteen

Leah would never forget those days immediately after the revolution. She and all her friends went out into the streets, joining the throngs there. Soldiers in drab and olive, horsemen in blue and gold, white-bloused sailors from the fleet, black-bloused workmen from the mills, girls in bright-colored dresses. On each marcher was a red flower, or a ribbon of red, or a scarlet kerchief about a woman's head. Red banners rippled in the wind.

Someone would strike up a revolutionary hymn; the deep, resonant voices of the soldiers would lift the refrain, joined by the plaintive voices of the working women. The hymn would rise, fall, die away, then down the line it would burst forth again, the whole street singing in harmony. Past the golden dome of St. Isaac Cathedral, past the minarets of the Mohamedan Mosque, marched forty creeds and races, joined into one by their enthusiasm for revolution.

Leah soon learned the words to the songs the people were singing, but when she had first heard the "Marseillaise," she had gotten a very strange feeling. The words, warped out of shape by Russian pronunciation, haunted her with their familiarity. "Radek," she had asked timidly, "aren't these words French?"

He had stopped and looked at her curiously. "Of course, the "Marseillaise" is the great anthem of the French Revolution."

"The French ... Revolution?" said Leah, thinking back to her peaceful life in Avignon. She waved her hand toward the marching crowds. "This has happened before?"

"Didn't you tell me when we first met that you were from France? No, don't worry about it. It doesn't matter. After meeting your gray friend there, I decided that maybe I didn't want to know exactly where you came from."

Something of the same feeling came to her when the workers talked about their enemies, the *burzhuy.* The professor had finally pronounced it correctly for her, bourgeoisie, the middle class, the capitalists. This was a French word, too. Many events must have transpired in Avignon after she had left. It gave her a strange feeling to know so little of what had happened during her leaps through time. It made her wish, at least a little, to have simply stayed where she was, to experience history as normal human beings did, a day at a time.

Ever since Scorpio had cured Radek with the orb, Radek had begun to look at her in an entirely new way. As if she and Scorpio were only two different species of alien.

Several weeks after the revolution, Leah was standing in a queue waiting for her turn to buy some sugar and bread, wondering why food was in even shorter supply now than it had been before. After the Tsar had been forced to abdicate, an interim government had formed under the leadership of Alexander Kerensky, and there was much talk about rebuilding society, but things had only gotten worse. Radek had believed that when the corrupt regime left power, things would instantly improve. The transformation from peasant to king was still a miracle to her, but she was beginning to realize that ingrained problems just didn't disappear that quickly.

From behind her, she heard a voice speak her name. When she turned, she recognized Maria Botchkareva, the woman soldier she had met on the train. Maria looked older, more tired, but she still had an indomitable look and still wore her soldier's gear. This time she was accompanied by two other women in uniform.

"I was surprised to see you alive and well," said Botchkareva. "I mean, I wondered what had happened to you since I left you in the city."

"A great many things have happened," said Leah, looking at the two other women soldiers, who appeared odd to her because their heads had been shaved and the hair had grown out only a little. She supposed it was the rule for recruits.

"And to me," said Botchkareva. "As you see, I've begun a training program for women." She displayed the black arrow symbol on her sleeve. "The Battalion of Death."

"Not exactly a comforting name," said Leah.

"There are other Death Battalions," said Botchkareva. "It only means extreme patriotism, to battle to the death, if need be."

"I was surprised to see the war continue," said Leah, "after all that happened here."

"Of course the war must continue," said Botchkareva. "The head of the Provisional Government gave me the authority to train these women for combat, but there is a problem, and I'm on my way to consult with him about a matter of some importance."

"Alexander Kerensky? You know him?"

"Yes, you may come along, if you want to meet him, but you'll have to pretend to be one of my recruits."

"All right, if it doesn't have to be too realistic," said Leah, touching her own long hair nervously.

The recruits laughed and accompanied her to a rest room, where they provided an extra uniform for her out of their duffel bags and helped her pin up her hair under a soldier's cap. "This isn't going to be a peaceful meeting," said one of them. "Botchkareva, our *nachalnik*, hasn't been happy ever since she heard of Order Number One."

When Leah looked puzzled, the girl explained, "When the soldiers took over Petrograd, they influenced the Petrograd legislative body, the Duma, to pass Order Number One. It gave each regiment and company the right of self-government, through a Soviet of Soldier's Deputies. It was first just for the city garrisons, but soon spread to the German front."

"Self-government sounds only fair."

"Don't let the *nachalnik* hear you say that," said the girl. Leah found the mirror and gazed at her distinctly less feminine figure. An olive-drab uniform with her hair hidden under the cap completely changed her appearance.

"You look quite handsome," said the other recruit. "Maybe we'll have a new volunteer for our Battalion?"

"I'd have to do some hard thinking before I joined anything called the Battalion of Death," said Leah, laughing. The others joined in good-naturedly.

The Provisional Government had taken over the Tauride Palace for its headquarters. As she entered the place, Leah heard the cadence of voices, rising and falling, making a point or disagreeing. They passed by the meeting room where the ministers sat around long tables, carrying on what seemed an interminable argument. *So many problems*, she thought.

They found Kerensky in an office converted from some aristocrat's suite. Heavy blood-red velour drapes with gilt fringe hung at the windows, and a frieze of sculpture followed one wall, the double-headed eagle design still prominent. The signs of nobility were still there, Leah realized, built so solidly into the architecture that it might be decades before they were totally gone.

A simple desk and chair had been commandeered from somewhere, and as they were announced, Kerensky rose to meet them. He was tall, five feet eight or so and his thick brown hair bristled in a pompadour. His face was deeply lined and pale, almost an ashen gray, as if he had been ill. He had a large nose, a deeply curved mouth and a strong cleft chin. He looked weary now, his eyes a brooding and somber gray.

"I refuse to allow my Women's Brigade to form a Soviet and hold meetings," Botchkareva was saying.

"But self-government for all soldiers is now the law," said Kerensky.

"Revolution and self-government is all very well here," said Botchkareva, "but it makes no sense in war where the troops and officers must trust each other to survive. I have heard of soldiers on the front lines who held meetings and decided not to follow officers they didn't like. Worse, I've seen them kill their officers. Especially now when you have declared that there will be no capital punishment for soldiers. We cannot fight a war under such conditions!"

"I didn't give you permission to train a Women's Brigade so you could go against my orders," said Kerensky. "If you do not wish to continue the project, I'm sure someone else can be found."

"Very well, I will resign."

"All the women will resign with you, *Nachalnik,*" said a recruit. "That is the way we feel. There will be no Women's Brigade."

"Be reasonable," said Kerensky. "The project has been successful so far. We need every advantage we can get if we want to win this war."

"No meetings for my troops," said Botchkareva.

"You will obey my orders or I'll have you shot!" said Kerensky. Anger made him throw off his weariness. His eyes, deep in their sockets, burned with somber fires and his voice, at first soft and cajoling, now blazed with the intensity and precision of machine-gun fire. Leah could see how his commanding presence and distinctive voice had quickly brought him to the forefront of the Provisional Government.

Yet she couldn't help comparing him to Lenin, not entirely favorably. She felt that, in Kerensky, perhaps style outpaced substance, especially since it was obvious he had forgotten his own edict against capital punishment for soldiers.

Glad to be back in her own clothes again, Leah said good luck to Botchkareva and waved goodbye to the women soldiers. She hadn't gone very far when she heard the squawking noise she now easily recognized as the honking of a motor car's horn. Pugatchev veered over toward the curb where she stood.

"I'm supposed to come and collect you," he said rapidly. "Radek has a new project in the works. He's so excited about it, I think I'll let him tell you."

Instead of returning to their hotel, Pugatchev drove up before an almost featureless gray stone building with only a small brass plaque on the side. Leah read the words as Pugatchev hurried her past: *Nashe Slovo.* It meant "Our Word," but what the building contained, she couldn't guess.

Pugatchev led her past a series of offices that looked as if someone had run riot through them, overturning desks, scattering chairs, making a pile of papers and setting fire to them. Luckily someone must have doused the fire with water before it took hold. Quite a few buildings were gutted by fire because of the revolutionaries' enthusiasm.

She found Radek in a large room, standing before an immense machine that was vaguely familiar in form. After a moment she realized that it was a printing press, though a good deal larger and more complicated-looking than Radek's had been.

"Some friends of mine captured this place," said Radek, "and turned it over to me so that I can get it back into operation. The whole country is hungry for news. I'm going to rename the paper *Narodny Slovo*, the 'People's Word,' in honor of the revolutionary movement."

"This is wonderful," said Leah. She walked around the press and admired it. "No more hiding and printing secret tracts."

"Yes, we'll get things rolling very soon. We're a little shorthanded, though. I'm not sure exactly what we'll print."

"Who were those three you were with when I found you?" asked Pugatchev idly. "There was something strange about them. I couldn't quite figure out what."

"That was an acquaintance of mine, Maria Botchkareva and two recruits to her Women's Brigade. We had just been to the Tauride Palace to talk to Kerensky about the war."

I thought their uniforms looked funny," said Pugatchev. "I mean, well—"

Radek gaped at her. "Quickly, you must tell me everything about them, everything that happened!"

Leah sat down and told him what had occurred, while he asked questions to fill in this or that detail, all the while taking notes on a pad.

"This is a wonderful news story," he said when she had finished. "Can you get more news?"

"Well, I don't know. That depends on what is meant by news."

"Well, I don't know ... important things ... about important people ... exciting happenings. And of course the best news is always something that no one knows about yet."

"I think I see."

"I'm very shorthanded here. You must try, while Stefan and I get the press ready." He rushed away, leaving Leah standing there puzzled.

"I think I know what he means by news," she said, "but how am I supposed to know where these things are taking place?"

"I know of one event you might cover," said Pugatchev. "Lenin is returning to Petrograd tonight. His followers and the Provisional Government have arranged a welcome for him at the Finland Station."

Scorpio sat in Professor Mirskaya's new flat, staring out of the window at a pair of Red Guards, warming themselves over a fire built in an oil drum. He had been told that these workers with rifles had organized themselves spontaneously during earlier uprisings. The guns slung across their shoulders reminded him that this was a violent place. As if he needed reminding.

After discovering the Hunter's death, he had been in a deep depression. Leah and the professor had both talked to him, telling him that Ardon's death wasn't his fault, but the Aquay were nonaggressive by nature. It was painfully obvious to him that if he hadn't led Ardon to this time, the Hunter would not have been locked in that awful hole. He would not have died at the hands of these humans. Some of his best friends were humans now, he supposed, but it was hard to overlook several glaring faults in the race, one of them being a propensity to murder each other.

After a while, he made an effort to draw himself out of these bleak thoughts. It was sad about Ardon, but there was really nothing he could do about it now. The Tsarevitch, on the other hand, was still ill. He took out the orb and stood staring at it.

"I thought you were feeling too low to want to continue our experiments today," said the professor, looking up from her paperwork.

"I was, but I remembered that I'd more or less promised to see what I could do about the Tsarevitch's illness."

"Alexei is no longer the Tsarevitch," said the professor gently. "Nicholas and his family are under house arrest at Tsarskoe Selo."

"Guards can't keep me out," said Scorpio.

"No, but think. The Tsar and his family are already in enough trouble. The sight of an intruder might make the guards so nervous that they would shoot indiscriminately. Alexei or one of his family might be hurt by accident."

"Then what's the use of this thing?" said Scorpio, holding out the orb. "If it couldn't protect Ardon and it can't help me heal Alexei, then how do I know it will be of any help at all in rescuing my people? Maybe it will only take me back home in time to watch the last of my race be killed."

"The use of the 'thing' is what we were trying to learn," said the professor, "before you got so emotional. Science is neither morality nor wish fulfillment. We simply find out because we must know."

"I suppose you're right," said Scorpio with a sigh. "And perhaps I'm ready now to continue our experiments."

Chapter Fifteen

Lethor chuckled as he ran down the street, thinking of how surprised the peacekeepers had looked when the Hunters had used their lasers. With Hunter speed and endurance, they would soon outdistance any peacekeepers foolish enough to give chase.

When he thought he'd gone far enough, he slowed his pace, giving Ardon plenty of time to catch up. Then he stopped and looked back. No one was on the street behind him. He could hardly believe that the peacekeepers with their weak bodies and outmoded projectile weapons could have stopped a Beta. There had been quite a few of them, he remembered, with more coming in as he jumped through the window. It simply hadn't occurred to him that Ardon wouldn't be right behind.

If the orb had recovered, he could go back quickly and see what had happened. Taking the orb out of its pouch, he looked at it.

It was pale and withered-looking, and no radiance shone from it, even though he shook it, hard. At first a natural arrogance protected him from realizing the meaning of the orb's loss. But as he stared at the Petrograd street filled with frozen snow and dirty slush plowed up by passing vehicles, it began to occur to him that this place, with its frozen moisture falling from the sky to burn the skin, its freezing temperatures and its stupid, stolid indigenes, would become his only reality. To escape from that thought, he turned around and went back the way he had come.

He didn't need to approach too closely to the building where the peacekeepers had attacked them because his nearvision allowed him to see the convoy that left. Ardon, in chains, marched along with two other prisoners. There were many guards with bayonets—too many, he finally decided, to risk any sort of attack.

He trailed along behind them until they reached the long bridge, then he could follow no longer for fear of drawing too much attention to himself. Lethor knew that Ardon, like all Betas, had perfect trust in his leader. He would be waiting to be rescued.

The problem was that at the moment Lethor had no plan for such a rescue. Being alone was a new and confusing experience. He wasn't capable of missing Ardon in the way one human missed another; it was more like the sensation of trying to reach for things with a missing hand. It simply had never occurred to him that Ardon wouldn't be there.

Several days later Lethor made his way cautiously down a street of what had been fine houses. Now most of them had a derelict look. Snow was beginning to fall from a meanlooking sky, a frigid wind whipping snowflakes into his face. It was as if he were the target of a thousand tiny stinging insects, his skin burning as the snowflakes melted; he needed shelter badly.

Rags of curtains flapped from broken windows like flags of truce. He stood there, uncertain. A few days ago a plague of insanity had broken out among the natives. They had begun to act erratically, to roam the streets in unruly mobs, using their projectile weapons on one another. Lethor had very nearly been killed by a sniper firing at random from the top of a building.

Young Hunters sometimes were afflicted by what was called blood-madness when they made their first kills, but nothing in Lethor's experience prepared him for what had happened here. Hunters knew a great deal about killing, but nothing of war. Their numbers had always been relatively small, so there was no competition for territory. From birth, a Hunter fulfilled only one role in society. A Beta could not aspire to become an Alpha; that was nonsense.

A Hunter's weapons were designed for the single kill, because according to their code, it was unthinkable to mow down a thousand to bring down one individual.

He supposed he would never know why these humans had lost their minds, though it was probably because those minds were terribly weak to begin with. For his purposes, he didn't really care, except that he didn't want to become a casualty.

As he stared at the house, focusing on the windows with his near-vision, he saw no signs of life within. This structure must have been abandoned by its owners when the craziness broke out, and should be safe enough for the night. He hadn't imagined that finding shelter and food could be such huge problems. Before, it had been easy to appear someplace, take what was needed and disappear again, before the alarm could be sounded. The useless orb in its pouch swung against his ribs as he mounted the front steps.

Fragments of the door still hung in the doorway like wooden fangs. Lethor grasped these and wrenched them off, and then ducked to go inside. It was not warm; he could still see the plume of his breath, but at least the horde of stinging snowflakes could not follow him here. The room was in disarray, furniture tumbled and broken. Clotted mud smeared the polished wooden floors, as if muddy boots had tracked across them. Baubles valued by the indigenes, such as yellow metal candlesticks, canvases daubed with colored pigments and strings of glittering stones, lay abandoned on the floor, as if looting had suddenly been interrupted. That made Lethor feel nervous, but he didn't want to go outside again. And now that he had shelter, hunger was beginning to make his belly feel pinched. He kicked the valuables aside as he crossed the room, hoping that whoever had fled had left a full larder.

Only the razor-edged reflexes trained into him early saved his life. A subliminal sound made him throw himself sideways just as the weapon went off with a crack, the projectile burying itself in the wall before him. His nerves had been on edge all day. Now he whirled and fired upward into the darkness in the direction from which the shot had come. In the light from his weapon's beam, he saw a strange vision: one of the natives, a female, bulky in several layers of clothing as if she had put her whole wardrobe on at once, hair uncombed and standing out wildly, a tiara of the glittering stones set askew on her head. But it was her eyes that made him want to flee. She knelt above him on the staircase, long-barreled pistol clutched in both hands and braced against the banister.

"I knew you'd come back for the valuables!" she shouted. "Peasant scum! I'll kill as many of you as I can before I die!" Lethor hit the floor as she fired again. He lifted his own weapon. This female wasn't proper prey, but she was making a nuisance of herself.

"Take my jewelry, my paintings!" she shrieked, firing again. His second shot, well calculated, hit the banister cutting it in two. The female, who had been leaning against it, fell amid her valuables with a thump, the pistol skittering out of reach across the polished floor.

Lethor looked anxiously toward the back of the house. It was possible there was food here. On the other hand, he had seen armed patrols on the march through these streets, and the shots the female had fired were sure to bring them on the run. He didn't want to be trapped inside. The female native sat up dazedly. As he went out, she scrabbled through the wreckage for her pistol. She would probably lie in wait for the next intruder, but it hardly mattered to him.

Discouraged, Lethor continued his travels in search of food and shelter. As he rounded a corner, he heard shouts, pistol shots, and saw several shadowy shapes dart from a doorway, carrying sacks slung over their shoulders. Looters more successful than himself he decided. On impulse, he trotted along in the direction they had gone, thinking that perhaps in their night's hunting something might be left for him. It didn't escape him that he was playing the part of scavenger now, not of Hunter, but he was hungry and tired enough not to care. He would gratefully take whatever he could get now.

The looters moved out of the more affluent districts, making detours whenever they saw armed patrols, and entered a slum. As they did, their pace slackened. Lethor could hear them laughing and joking together. Their hunting had been good.

When they climbed under the overhang of a bridge, he caught the intermittent glow of a fire. The looters must have established a temporary camp here. Cautiously, Lethor moved closer. It was dark, and if he kept his face covered, they might take him for a human.

"Ho, stranger," called out a hoarse voice. "What are you doing here?" Lethor counted nine silhouettes against the leaping firelight. He knew that some of these men were armed. He suspected all were insane, like the female in the house. He doubted he could kill all of them before they swarmed over him.

A rich meaty aroma came from something they were cooking in a dented kettle over the fire.

Lethor modulated his voice to a dry whisper, which was the closest he could come to sounding human. "Just like you," he said. "Taking what I can get. But for me, hunting hasn't been good. May I share a corner of your shelter and perhaps a bite of food?" Lethor could hardly believe himself capable of speaking these words.

One man laughed raucously. "Do we look like a charity?"

"Shut up, Karpov," said the man who had spoken first. "We all shared what we had to make the stew, stranger. If you have something to add to it, you are welcome. Otherwise, move on."

As Lethor turned away, the orb in its pouch brushed his side again. *Worthless thing*, he thought. And then he thought again. Removing the orb, he held it out. "This is all I have."

"A half-rotten potato," said Karpov.

"I'm a man of my word," the second man said. "I will add it to the kettle and you may share."

Lethor thought the man looked at him suspiciously when he came close enough to take the orb. They would soon realize that he wasn't of their kind, but Lethor hoped it was after he had had a chance to eat something.

The man held the orb over the steaming kettle a moment and then dropped it in. And that was that, thought Lethor, trying not to think of repeating this indignity night after night. It seemed rather more likely that these crazy natives would kill him before too many days had passed.

A burst of incandescence shot out of the kettle, making the circle of men around it jump backward in surprise. Lethor raced up and saw the orb, now glowing a rich gold, floated lightly on the surface of the boiling water. Quickly he snatched it up and began to run before the looters could recover.

It's alive again, he thought. It must have been the cold, all along. The heat thawed it out. He stopped. But why am I running, when I have the orb?

He cupped his hands around it and jumped.

Eager to recover his companion, he emerged in the courtyard of one of the cell complexes of the Fortress. Everything was in confusion here. Some cell doors stood open. The guards themselves were so busy fleeing, they hardly had time to acknowledge his sudden appearance. He blocked the way of a hurrying guard, then grabbed him by the front of his uniform when he tried to dodge away.

"Wha-what are you?" stammered the guard.

"Yes, look at me well," said Lethor, pushing back his hat so that his captive got a really good look. "There was another like me imprisoned here. Where is he kept?"

"I have seen nothing like you before," affirmed the guard, though Lethor could see that he lied.

"Where is he?" asked Lethor, giving his captive a hard shake for each individual word.

"I think he was in cell eight, but many of the cells in the Alexis Ravelin are empty. We've been under siege and are just about to surrender. Since it doesn't matter anymore, some of us just opened the cell doors and let the prisoners go free."

"Lead me there. I want to see," said Lethor, and dragged the poor guard along with him. Cell number eight was indeed empty. Lethor stepped into the dank, cramped room, instantly feeling the claustrophobia of his desert-dwelling race. Quickly he stepped out again.

"I may have seen him in here, but I don't know where he's gone. Red Guards will soon be overrunning this place, so you'd better get out while you can."

Seeing that the man was now telling the truth, Lethor loosened his grip. "Who does know? Who's in charge here?"

"I think the higher officers fled, but someone may still be in the commander's office." He indicated a large grey stone building at the center of the complex. The guard was still begging to be released when Lethor orb-hopped.

The commander's office was in disarray. One soldier was shouting into a communications device; his comrade was dumping the contents of filing cabinets onto the floor and setting them on fire. He chose the man who was destroying records and let the other one drop the communications device and escape. "Are you in charge here?" he asked.

The soldier's attention was on setting the fire. He hadn't seen Lethor appear. "Does it look like I'm in charge of anything?" asked the soldier, without turning to see who he addressed.

When he did turn, he gaped at Lethor. "You—but you're dead!"

"I'm very much alive," said Lethor, blocking the man's way when he tried to run. Behind the soldier, flames rose out of the stacks of papers; Lethor thought that feeling the heat of it on his back might make the man more cooperative. "But why would you think I was dead. Have you seen someone like me before?"

"Please, the fire—" begged the man, looking over his shoulder to see the rising flames.

Lethor didn't move.

"Yes, someone like you in cell number eight. He died one night under mysterious circumstances."

"He was dead. You're sure? What was done with his body?"

"Well, I was told the body disappeared. No trace of it remained." Again the man looked nervously at the fire. Small runners of flame had almost reached his feet.

As the man spoke, Lethor studied his expressions. He told the truth. Ardon was dead and no trace of his body remained.

Lethor had a feeling that among the burning records was the whole truth about Ardon's death, but he didn't really need to know any more. He let go of the soldier, who ran for the exit.

My companion is dead, he thought with a definite emphasis on his own loss. Trying to bond with and train a new Beta would be like learning to grasp with an artificial hand. Ardon was irreplaceable.

Despite the Aquays' reputation for nonviolence, Scorpio must have used his orb to travel here, and finding Ardon locked up and weaponless, he murdered him. Only an orb would make the body seem to disappear without a trace. *I took a Hunter's oath that I would kill the Aquay before returning home, but what has been taken from me makes it more personal.* Flames were rising all around Lethor singeing his sheepskin coat. A moment later he activated the orb and was gone.

Chapter Sixteen

The crowd in front of the Finland Station blocked the whole square, scarcely letting the trams through. Military bands marched and played beneath red flags and banners. There was a roar of many motor cars and in two or three places the bulky outlines of armored cars thrust up from the crowd. And from one of the side streets, startling the mob and cutting through it, moved a mounted searchlight, which abruptly projected images upon the darkness: strips of the city, the roofs, many-storied houses, columns, wires, tramways and human figures.

Somehow Leah made her way through the surging mob outside, but there was an even greater crush inside the station: more delegations, flags and sentries demanding to see one's authorization for going farther. Radek had given her a press pass from the old *Nashe Slovo.* They didn't seem to realize it was no more and allowed Leah to enter. The former Imperial Waiting Room with its glass doors gave a good view of the platform, and a group of dignitaries had been assembled here for the official welcome.

She saw that the platform was even more impressive than the square, its whole length lined with people, mostly soldiers waiting to present arms. Triumphal arches festooned with red and gold had been set up and banners proclaimed every sort of revolutionary slogan. At the end of the platform, where the carriage was expected to stop, stood a band and several people holding immense bouquets of flowers.

The train pulled in, and the band's spirited playing of the "Marseillaise" filtered in through closed doors. Someone was shouting, "Make way there, comrades! Please, make way!" and Lenin came hurrying into the room. He was wearing a round cap, his cheeks were ruddy with cold and he carried a magnificent bouquet, which contrasted strangely with his whole appearance.

The representative from the Provisional Government delivered a solemn speech, welcoming Lenin, but emphasizing that all parties should close ranks and work together to build a new society.

Lenin stood nonchalantly, as if nothing taking place had the slightest connection with him. He looked about him, examining people in the crowd and the ceiling of the Imperial Waiting Room, rearranging his bouquet, then, turning away from the official delegation toward the crowd, he made his reply.

"Comrades: soldiers, sailors, workers! The hour is not far distant when the peoples of the world will turn their arms against their own capitalist exploiters. The worldwide Socialist revolution has already dawned. The Russian revolution has prepared the way and opened a new epoch. Long live the worldwide Socialist revolution!"

The crowd roared approval. Leah was intrigued. Not only had Lenin just refused to support the Provisional Government, he considered all that had already happened only a prologue for what was to occur worldwide.

The official welcome over, the crowd outside began trying to break through the glass doors from the square. Again a way was cleared for Lenin. The "Marseillaise" was played again, and through cheering throngs and red and gold banners sporadically illuminated by the searchlight, Lenin went out through the main entrance and was about to enter a closed car. The crowd refused to allow this and he climbed onto the hood of the car to make a speech. Leah heard the echoes:

"Capitalist pirates … worldwide Socialist Revolution …"

• • •

Though it was late, she returned to the newspaper office, terribly impressed and ready to convey what she had seen and felt to Radek, but she found him sitting slumped behind the desk in the editor's office, his head resting on his hands, as if he were unutterably weary. When she described the preparations at the station, he said, "That is nothing. Lenin's party, the Bolsheviks, excel at organization and know how to put on a good show. You really didn't suppose all that was spontaneous, did you?"

"Even if it wasn't, it was still spectacular, but it wasn't so much that, it's that we thought everything had been settled by the formation of the Provisional Government."

"It has been. The Bolsheviks are still in the minority. They can do nothing."

"But what about the worldwide Socialist revolution that is to come? Surely that must be news."

Radek yawned. "Propaganda isn't news. I'm surprised you even half believed it."

"So I battled my way through a mob and you won't print any of this?"

"I won't because I can't," sighed Radek. "Come with me.

The huge press that she had marveled at before sat still and silent. No river of freshly printed pages poured from its maw. It occupied the center of the room like a brooding, complex idol whose worshipers had fled.

Radek had been so sure he would have it working by now. "Is it broken?" Leah asked.

"No, it's in perfect working condition. The problem is a shortage of paper. It seems that shipments haven't come into the city for several months now. The transportation of goods is even more erratic now than it was under the tsars." He laughed softly. "It's almost funny. We are a generation that learned only how to disrupt things. Now that the time has come to put things back together again, we find ourselves totally inept."

"Is there no chance that you can get it running?"

"Well, Pugatchev and some others are scouring the city for paper. You know how resourceful he can be, so maybe there's a small chance."

"In that case I'll go out and find a story you'll want to print," said Leah.

"Fine. As long as it is not about that upstart Lenin. I'll be glad when his name sinks back into the obscurity it deserves."

The next morning, determined to get something Radek would consider news, Leah went to the professor's flat to see Scorpio.

"How are your experiments going?" she asked, feeling guilty that she had been so wrapped up in her revolutionary activities that she didn't know how Scorpio was faring.

"We continue to make progress," said Scorpio.

"I have a favor to ask. I'm gathering news for Radek's newspaper, the *Narodny Slovo*, and he tells me that the best news is that which no one knows about yet."

The skin of the orb thinned and dissolved, leaving Leah and Scorpio on a Petrograd street that she soon recognized by the landmarks as the Nevsky. It was night, but only a few arc lights illuminated the pavement. People were hurrying in all directions, moving shadows thrown large against the sides of buildings. A hollow booming sound made Leah jump. "What's that?" she asked of a passerby.

"Those are the guns of the Aurora, firing on the Winter Palace," he called out over his shoulder. "You'd better take cover, the Bolsheviks are making their move tonight against the Provisional Government."

"At last. I think we've found our story," said Leah. Scorpio had manned the orb, making several stops along the way, so that Leah could determine whether anything newsworthy was happening. On one of these short stops, she had been told that the Provisional Government was now housed in the Winter Palace.

"I'm still not so sure this was a good idea," said Scorpio.

"But you said you didn't think there'd be any problem of returning to our point of departure, and the professor seemed to think this was a fine idea."

"You'll notice the professor hasn't been a passenger of the orb herself since she escaped the Fortress. Still, I *believe* I can return us to the moment from which we left. In this case the Ubiquity Effect doesn't apply because we are in no danger of meeting a second version of ourselves, as long as—"

"We'd better hurry if we want to see what's happening," interrupted Leah.

Beyond the pale discs thrown by the street lamps it was totally dark. Leah could see soldiers moving here and there, standing in doorways conferring. In front of the Kazan Cathedral a three-inch field gun lay askew in the street, where its recoil must have thrown it after its last firing. She noted that in command of each patrol of regular army was a Red Guard.

Anonymous in darkness, Leah and Scorpio joined the throngs of soldiers moving silently down the street toward the Winter Palace. As they crowded through the Red Arch, someone shouted, "Look out, comrades. They may be waiting for us!" Stooping low and running in a zigzag pattern, Leah and Scorpio crossed the open space, ducking behind the Alexander column. All around them the soldiers moved forward silently, without any orders. In the light coming from the windows of the palace Leah saw that the first few hundred men were Red Guards, with only a few scattered members of the regular army. Oddly enough they met no defense. On both sides of the main gateway the doors stood wide open with light streaming out, but not a sound came from within.

"This way," said Scorpio as they ran inside and were confronted by an immense vaulted room from which issued a maze of corridors. They passed *Yunkers*, soldiers from officer's training school, and members of the Women's Battalion coming out with hands up, in bunches of three or four. The invaders seized them and shook them about, but only took their weapons and marched them away without further violence.

Several Red Guards with fixed bayonets appeared in the door, waving the crowd aside. After them followed in single file half a dozen men in civilian dress: the members of the Provisional Government under arrest.

"Where is Kerensky?" came several shouts.

"He escaped in his car before all this started," answered a Red Guard. There were answering catcalls and curses at this news.

Surprised that no one questioned or stopped them, Leah and Scorpio found themselves in a large ornate room with gilded cornices and enormous crystal lusters, and beyond it several smaller rooms, wainscoted with dark wood. On both sides of the parquete floor lay rows of dirty mattresses and blankets. Everywhere was a litter of cigarette butts, bits of bread crust and empty bottles with expensive French labels. The place had been a barracks for weeks, from the looks of it, and machine guns were mounted on windowsills, rifles stacked between the mattresses.

As Leah and Scorpio continued to walk through the palace, unnoted in the confusion, they saw soldiers moving here and there through the vast structure, looking for remaining nests of *Yunkers* and members of the Women's Battalion. The paintings, statues, tapestries and carpets of the State apartments were all in place, but in the living quarters, beds had been stripped and wardrobes were empty. The offices had been ransacked, the contents of desks and cabinets turned out onto the floor. They saw old palace servants standing about helplessly, occasionally admonishing a soldier out of habit, "You can't enter there, *barm.* It is forbidden!"

When they reached the chamber where the ministers had been in session, an opulent room in gold and malachite with crimson brocade hangings, they saw the long tables covered in green baize just as the ministers had left them. Pen and ink and paper were still set before each empty chair. The papers were filled with the beginnings of speeches and proclamations that became only mindless doodles as they had evidently waited, without hope, for the Bolsheviks to attack.

"It's over," said Leah softly. "Lenin has won after all."

• • •

On the same evening Vasha and Misha wandered the streets of Petrograd with the crowds, neither of them quite certain what all these happenings meant to them personally, though they enjoyed the excitement, the carnival atmosphere. The jeweler who had hired them earlier had taken his wares and fled during the early rioting; down the Nevsky was blazed a trail of shattered windows and looted shops. Armored cars with sirens screaming and red flags flying from the turrets, crammed with soldiers, bayonets jutting on every side, dashed by. Stretched full-length on the car fenders lay sharpshooters, rifles projecting beyond the lamps, eyes on the watch for provocators.

The atmosphere made Vasha feel adventurous, and as they joined the mob converging upon the palace, he said to his brother, "Now that the revolution has come, doesn't that mean that all of us should share in the wealth, to live like tsars ourselves?"

Misha laughed. "Brother, you must've drunk too much vodka."

"No, it's true, I tell you." He gestured toward the facade of the palace, pale green and gold, its tall windows blazing with light.

"The soldiers would only chase us away," said Misha.

"Let's find out."

Losing themselves in a crowd surging through the gate, they were swept into the right-hand entrance.

"You see, we are the new owners," said Vasha as they went inside. "That was what the revolution was all about, giving folk such as ourselves our just due. It was obvious that you and I were too good for the menial jobs we could get from the *burzhuy.*"

"Looks like someone else got the idea first," said Misha. There were obvious signs of looting. Broken bits of furniture littered the floor, and large paintings had been slashed from their frames.

"But look at the size of this place. There must be plenty more left, somewhere," said Vasha, and led the way into a corridor with doorways to either side. Through one of these doors, Vasha saw what he had been seeking: several trunks and crates pushed against the wall. He led his brother to them.

When he pried open the top of a crate, he found treasure: several soft, thick blankets with the royal crest worked into them, an ornate, gilded clock and who knew what else. He pulled out one of the blankets and wrapped it about himself. "These will keep us warm these bitter nights," he said, tossing another one to Misha. "And this will sell for a goodly sum." He put the clock on his shoulder and danced it around.

"You were right, Vasha, we're going to return to Tutal-sk as rich men!" Misha delved into the crate himself.

"Ho, comrades," came a voice from the doorway. "What are you doing?" A small, thin man in the uniform of the Red Guard came into the room behind them.

"We've found a treasure trove, courtesy of the Tsar," said Vasha. "Come in and share with us. There's plenty for all."

"Shame, comrades," said the man. "Don't you know that all property here is now the property of the people." He grabbed the end of the blanket and attempted to pull it from Vasha's shoulders. Vasha pulled back and for a few minutes they had a tug-of-war. The clock fell from Vasha's shoulder and smashed on the parquetry. Misha, seeing his brother being accosted by a stranger, joined the fight and all three of them were pulling on the blanket in opposite directions. Finally, the soldier called for help and others came running.

"These men are stealing from the people," he shouted, and others took up the cry. "Put everything back. Don't take anything. Property of the people!"

Three soldiers quickly pulled the blanket away from Vasha. They grabbed both of the brothers roughly and hauled them out into the corridor where two Red Guards, a soldier and an officer, sat at a table with pen and paper making lists. All items that had been taken away from looters were piled on the floor: statuettes, bottles of ink, candles, cakes of soap, clothing.

As the soldiers searched the pockets of Vasha and Misha to make sure they hadn't taken any smaller trinkets, they explained that stealing was unworthy of liberators of the people. Then they marched them outside.

"These things belong to all the people now," said the worker. "Nothing goes out of the palace tonight."

"Property of the people," said Vasha in disgust as they walked away. "I thought we *were* the people."

"We were happier hunting wolves in Tutalsk," said Misha. "I don't understand revolutions. Let's go home."

Vasha looked at his brother. He didn't like to admit it, but occasionally the little onion head got a good idea. "I think you might be right, Misha," he said, "but we have no money left."

"Maybe you don't, but I do," said Misha. "I saved part of my money every week, hoping that eventually you'd come back to your senses."

"Why didn't you tell me this sooner. Let's go back to Tutalsk where things are not so crazy."

The two brothers linked arms and walked together down the street.

Scorpio seemed quite happy as the orb appeared before the newspaper office. "I think I'm finally gaining control," he said. "Since I've seen nothing of Lethor, there should be plenty of time to continue my experiments with Professor Mirskaya."

"What do you suppose happened to him?" asked Leah.

"Things have been rather unsettled here. Something unfortunate might have befallen him," said Scorpio. "I'd rather not speculate."

Leah looked around suspiciously, wondering if this were really the approximate time they had left. The newspaper office looked as it had before, and when she asked a passerby for the date, everything seemed to have gone as planned. Something still nagged at the corners of her mind; something she had overlooked.

As they went inside, Leah heard a familiar and welcome sound, the metallic clatter of a printing press. Radek ran up to her as she entered, and forgetting himself, embraced her impulsively.

"We managed to find a shipment of paper," he said, "and are getting out an issue. We can also do the next few issues, but I'm not sure what happens after that. I hope you've been working on that big story you promised!"

"Well, I, uh, about that," stammered Leah.

Radek looked at her hopefully.

"I went everywhere," she said, "but there was nothing worth reporting. I'm sorry."

"Never mind, we'll come up with something for tomorrow's edition."

Leah wasn't sure why she had faltered when the moment came to tell Radek how his revolution had come out. It was not only that she knew he wouldn't be pleased with the outcome; she realized that it was so much *his* revolution that he probably wouldn't have believed her anyway. She took out the folded and yellowed piece of paper with Nechayev's revolutionary catechism on it and tucked it back into his pocket.

"Why are you returning that?"

"I've read it until I understand it," she said, remembering the words: "All the soft and tender affections arising from kinship, friendship and love ... must be obliterated."

She gave him a light, friendly kiss. *I hope you won't be able to obliterate me entirely*, she thought.

They heard a commotion in the outside offices, shouts, the sounds of a fight and then a bulky shape appeared in the doorway. Though the figure wore the sheepskin coat of a peasant, it had no hat and they could see that Lethor had finally caught up to them. The skin of his face was split and cracked and his clothing was grimy, as if he'd had a very bad time of it up to now, but when he saw them, his face was suffused with a look of wicked delight.

"What is this?" said Radek, looking in confusion from Scorpio to the other alien.

Leah moved closer to Scorpio.

"I'm about to accord the two of you a great honor," said Lethor. "For centuries we Hunters have relied upon weapons to deal with prey, but because you murdered Ardon, I'm going to kill you both with my bare hands!"

Leah couldn't believe how fast the Hunter moved. With an almost casual sweep of his arm, he knocked Radek aside. In two bounds he crossed the room and reached for Leah and Scorpio. At the same time she felt something thrust into her hand.

Jump! she and Scorpio thought in unison.

The orb whisked them away.

In not-space, not-time, Leah's and Scorpio's thoughts meshed, the answers and the questions coming simultaneously.

"Did you hear Lethor say that I killed Ardon?" asked Scorpio in amazement.

"He must have been deranged. You saw his face."

"That might explain it, I suppose. But we risked our lives to find out how the revolution came out, and you didn't even tell Radek. Why?"

"I didn't believe he wanted to know. I think I realized that this was Radek's revolution, not mine. If I had decided to stay, I'd always be in competition with it. Now that I know poverty, ignorance and suffering aren't just something to be accepted, but something to struggle against, I have to find my own struggle among my own people. Anything else would feel wrong."

"I believe it is now possible to return to Avignon," said Scorpio. "As long as it is either before you were born or after you departed for the last time."

"But when Lethor came after us, you handed the orb to me, exactly as if you knew I'd be going with you."

"I did. Sort of. When you asked to jump into the future, I knew this was possible because we did so in Avignon. However, if you were going to stay in this time period, there was the possibility of meeting yourself. Therefore, if you were going to stay here, the orb would not have obeyed my command."

"You knew this and said nothing?"

"I was willing to accept things, either way," said Scorpio. "Don't be angry. When the orb allowed us to make the journey, I was happy because that meant our travels together weren't over, at least not right away."

"I'm not angry. I'm just happy to be going home."

The End of Book 3

Bibliography

Baron, Salo W. *The Russian Jew Under the Tsars and Soviets*. 2nd Edition. New York: The MacMillan Co., 1964.

Botchkareva, Maria. *Yashka: My Life as Peasant, Officer and Exile*. New York: Frederick A. Stokes Co., 1919.

Dorr, Reta Childe. *Inside the Russian Revolution*. New York: The MacMillan Co., 1917.

Gourko, General Basil. *War and Revolution*. New York: The MacMillan Co., 1919.

Heald, Edward Thornton. *Witness to Revolution*. Kent, OH: Kent State University Press, 1972.

Jermann, Edward. *Pictures From St. Petersburg*. New York: G.P. Putnam & Co., 1852.

Kaiser, Daniel H. *The Workers' Revolution in Russia: The View from Below*. Cambridge, New York: Cambridge University Press, 1987.

Payne, Robert. *The Fortress*. New York: Simon and Schuster, 1967.

Pethybridge, Roger. *Witness to the Russian Revolution*. London: Allen & Unwin, 1964.

Reed, John. *Ten Days that Shook the World*. New York: International Publishers, 1967.

Wiliams, Albert Rhys. *Journey into Revolution: Petrograd, 1917-1918*. Chicago: Quadrangle, 1969.

Williams, Albert Rhys. *Through the Russian Revolution*. New York: Boni & Livright, 1921.

SCORPIO
Dragon's Blood
Book 4

"This is certainly a peaceful place," observed Chan. "All the beasts living in harmony with each other. Maybe it really is a paradise."

They were just walking by a grove of spiky-leaved trees with trunks that looked like pineapples. Chan heard the crackling of something large displacing the foliage, and as he whirled around he saw a grotesque shape bearing down on him.

It was a huge lizardlike creature standing upright, though not erect, on heavily muscled rear legs. A long tail, held off the ground, balanced the weight of an enormous head. Its skin was green, darker on the back, set with small horny plates, the belly shading to ivory. Chan stood frozen, like someone in the path of an oncoming truck.

As he watched, the thing opened four-foot jaws. Its teeth were as long as knives . . .

For sales, editorial information, subsidiary rights information
or a catalog, please write or phone or e-mail

IBOOKS
Manhanset House
Shelter Island Hts., New York 11965, US
Tel: 212-427-7139
www.ibooksinc.com
bricktower@aol.com
www.IngramContent.com

For sales in the UK and Europe please contact our distributor,
Gazelle Book Services
White Cross Mills
Lancaster, LA1 4XS, UK
Tel: (01524) 68765 Fax: (01524) 63232
email: jacky@gazellebooks.co.uk

www.ingramcontent.com/pod-product-compliance
Lightning Source LLC
LaVergne TN
LVHW010613100826
845148LV00014B/2955

* 9 7 8 1 5 9 6 8 7 6 7 0 5 *